A Killer Christmas

The festivities are to die for...

LM Milford

Readthrough Press

The right of LM Milford to be identified as the author of this work has been asserted in accordance with the Copyright, Designs and Patents Act 1988.

All rights reserved. No part of this publication may be reproduced, stored in or transmitted into any retrieval system, in any form, or by any means (electronic , mechanical, photocopying, recording or otherwise) without the prior written permission of the publisher. Any person who does any unauthorised act in relation to this publication may be liable to criminal prosecution and civil claims for damages.

This is a work of fiction. Names, characters, business, places, events and incidents are either the products of the author's imagination or used in a fictitious manner. Any resemblance to actual persons, living or dead, or actual events is purely coincidental.

ISBN **9781913778187**

For my lovely husband Paul,
The person who always has my back and makes a fantastic cuppa

xx

Prologue

Just inside the back door of Fenleys department store, an overhead light flickered and buzzed. Fan heaters belched out hot air, making the inside of the shop uncomfortable, especially to someone in a winter coat. Fairy lights flashed in all directions, with different patterns on each of the many trees, and Slade yelled a reminder, if anyone needed it, that it was Christmas.

There were tables of Christmas goodies as far as the eye could see. Candy canes wrapped in cellophane, tins of biscuits and bars of chocolate that didn't really taste like chocolate. Even the homewares department had got in on the act with Santa-shaped cookie jars.

Christmas shoppers were conspicuous by their absence. Instead of a bustling, busy store, there was quiet. They were all gathered outside ready for the opening.

A figure stood by one wall, hidden behind the biggest tree, so still it could have been a mannequin modelling a thick jacket. Then movement, a glance at a watch. It was a waiting game; that was fine. The figure was no stranger to patience.

Another glance at the watch.

Then the doors slid open and a blast of cold air competed with the overhead heating. The figure shrank back as a man passed by, unaware that he was under scrutiny.

A hand went to a coat pocket. It was still there. Perfect.

The figure stepped forward. It was time.

Chapter one

'I can't believe you're dragging me into this.'

Emma Fletcher shivered in her thick winter coat and glared at Dan as they turned into the high street. She was out of breath, having been marched up the hill by Dan who was, for once, running late. That was her fault. She'd taken an age getting ready, hoping to keep out of the cold for as long as possible.

Dan squeezed her hand. 'You didn't have to come,' he said. 'I know jolly Christmas activities aren't your thing and you can probably think of better things to do on a Saturday afternoon, but Fenleys' Christmas window display opening is an event and I have to report on it.' He rubbed her arm. 'Plus, we promised Lydia we'd be here in support.'

Emma grumbled under her breath and Dan sighed heavily.

'I know you don't like her—'

'It's not a case of not liking her, it's that she doesn't like me. She's always looking down her nose at me.'

'You don't like her. That's fair enough,' Dan persisted, 'but we told Ed we'd be there. This is so much bigger than the book launch she organised earlier in the year. It sets the tone for the whole festive season.' He tugged on her arm.

'And it's got to be "the best Christmas ever"?' Emma asked, in a good impression of Lydia's plummy voice.

Dan laughed. 'You'll love it once you're there.'

'My feet are freezing,' Emma said, knowing she sounded whingy.

'Go straight to the pub then,' Dan said, now sounding slightly irritated. 'Me and Ed will meet you there.'

Emma shook her head. 'No, I'm here now. I might as well see the event for myself.'

Dan laughed. 'The Christmas spirit is coming to get you,' he said, digging her in the ribs.

She laughed and pushed him away, straightening the pink woolly hat she'd pulled over her red curly hair, making sure it was covering her ears.

The high street had been cordoned off to traffic and full of parents and excitedly chattering children, gathered outside the department store. It was just starting to get dark and the Christmas lights strung between lamp posts across the street automatically switched on. The families cheered loudly, making Emma jump.

'Right, I've got to get to work.' Dan turned and gave her a kiss on the lips. 'I won't be long.' He glanced around at the crowd and spotted a man waving at them. 'There's Ed,' he said, pointing.

Emma turned and waved back at Ed. 'OK, I'll be over there, see you in a bit.' She kissed him on the lips and watched as he approached a woman with two little girls in matching hats and scarves who were bouncing with anticipation.

'Hi, I'm Dan Sullivan from the *Allensbury Post*,' she heard him say. She turned away with a smile and began to weave her way through the crowd.

She arrived at Ed's side and grinned, pointing to his red beanie with an *Allensbury Post* logo on the front.

'I see the boss has branded you,' she said.

Ed grinned. 'I'm doing my bit by advertising,' he said, 'plus it's the warmest one I've got. I've been standing out here for over an hour.'

'An hour?' Emma squeaked.

Ed nodded. 'I came to give moral support as I was instructed, then Lydia said I was in the way so I went and got a coffee. Next I got a text asking where I'd gone and telling me to come back and look at the window.' He pointed towards the front of the department store where the window was hidden from view by a thick maroon curtain.

Emma frowned. 'You can't see anything from here,' she said.

Ed nodded and grimaced. 'I think Lydia forgot that in the stress of finalising things. I did get a peek from backstage though. It looks great.'

Emma tried not to visibly roll her eyes. 'And you've been out here for over an hour? Ed, you look frozen. Do you need more coffee?' Emma pointed towards the nearby Italian café.

Ed shook his head. 'I've managed to sneak off for another two since then. I'll never get to sleep tonight.' He puffed out his cheeks. 'I'll be glad when this is all over. It's all I've heard about for the last two months.'

'Not much longer,' Emma said, nudging him gently with her elbow. 'I'm buying the drinks when we're finished so that'll cheer you up.'

'Why are you buying the drinks?' Ed asked, looking surprised. 'I thought Dan would have to do it for freezing your feet.'

Emma laughed. 'No, I've whinged so much that I felt it was

only fair to make it up to him.'

Ed grinned. 'Where is the boy wonder?' he asked.

'Working his charm on everyone to get quotes for his story.'

'I thought being a crime reporter you'd have got out of attending things like this,' Ed said.

Emma shrugged. 'I'm here as moral support and to try and keep Dan calm. I swear he's more excited than the kids. I feel sorry for you sharing a flat with him.'

Ed laughed. 'The bauble and tinsel mountain is building and now that Fenleys' window is open he's allowed to put the tree up, apparently. All he needs now is an elf costume.'

Emma laughed and Dan appeared beside her. 'You two OK?' he asked, without looking up from the scribbles in his notebook. 'I swear the kids' names get weirder every year. I've had to check the spelling of every single name so far.'

Emma and Ed both laughed.

'At least I get a list of names printed out in the court papers,' Ed said. 'You get some weird and wonderful ones in there.'

Dan stowed his notebook in his coat pocket and dragged an *Allensbury Post* beanie hat from another pocket. He pulled it on and grinned at Ed.

'Another billboard,' he said. 'How's Lydia?'

'My assistance wasn't needed as early as it was thought,' Ed said. 'I've been out here mostly since I left the flat earlier.'

'Ooof, you must be freezing. Only a couple more minutes, mate,' Dan said. His mobile beeped and he checked the screen. 'Right, the photographer has what he needs so far and is in position at the front for the big moment.'

Suddenly a flurry of white flakes began to pour over the crowd. The families all cheered.

'Oh, for God's sake, Dan, it's bloody snowing.' Emma tried to disappear further into her coat. She looked up to see Dan and Ed grinning at her.

'It's a snow machine.' Ed pointed to the shop front. 'It's the signal that they're ready to start.'

A voice boomed over the tannoy system. 'Ladies and gentlemen, boys and girls, welcome to the opening of the Fenleys Winter Wonderland.' The crowd cheered. 'Please join me in a countdown. Ten, nine, eight...' The families began to chant the numbers. Dan joined in too, earning himself a dubious look from Emma, which made him laugh.

'Brace yourselves,' Ed said.

Emma pulled out her phone and clicked to camera mode.

'I knew it would get you,' Dan said.

'I might as well get a picture as I'm here. My mum will love it.' She still resented having to take off one of her fluffy pink gloves to operate the smartphone's screen.

The countdown reached zero and the red velvet curtains opened slowly. The families cheered louder and Emma snapped several photos. Then the cheers died away. Santa's grotto lay before them, with piles of fake snow and a line of stuffed reindeer, but the man himself was slumped sideways in his chair.

'Oh my God, do you think he's passed out drunk?' Emma asked, giggling, her gloved hand clasped to her mouth.

Dan laughed. 'Maybe he started on the sherry and mince pies a bit early.'

'Ho ho hammered?' Ed suggested and the other two groaned.

Lydia appeared in the window, looking flushed and angry. They saw her nudge Santa and the man tipped forward, falling off the chair onto the floor. Looking appalled, Lydia knelt beside him and shook his shoulder. She placed a hand on his back. Then she yanked her hand away. It was covered in a sticky red liquid.

Lydia's mouth fell open, her screams silenced by the thick glass. Several people in the crowd screamed as well and a child began to cry. Emma stared in shock, her gloved hand still covering her mouth.

'Oh my God, Dan, is he—?'

She turned to see Dan and Ed looking equally shocked. More children were crying now and the crowd seemed unable to move, transfixed by the scene in front of them.

The curtains swished back across the window, hiding the display.

Ed began to push his way through the crowd, closely followed by Emma and Dan.

'You were right,' Emma said, her voice shaking as much as her cold hands, unable to take her eyes off the curtained window in front of them. 'This certainly is an event.'

Chapter two

Dan pushed his way through the crowded bar of The Tavern, balancing two pints of lager and a large glass of Shiraz. He put them carefully down on the table. He sat down, and he and Ed watched Emma pacing outside the window, talking animatedly into her phone and reading from her notebook.

'I didn't know whether to get one for Lydia,' Dan said, pointing to the drinks. He glanced at his watch. 'She's been a long time.'

Ed lit up the screen of his phone. 'No word,' he said, turning to look towards the pub door again, as if that would conjure up his girlfriend.

'Don't worry, the police would have wanted to speak to everyone,' Dan said, taking a sip of his pint. 'There's quite a lot of people there. She knows where we are.'

There was a draught of cold air and a man shouted, 'Oi, put the wood in the hole,' to gales of laughter from his friends. Emma ignored him and threaded her way through the crowd of drinkers to their table.

'Did you see Lydia?' Ed asked, before Emma could even take

her coat off.

She shook her head. 'The police have got all the staff inside for questioning and they wouldn't give me any information. I spoke to a few of the parents who are still standing around outside. No one saw anything. I got some nice comments, people hoping that he's going to be OK. There's no ambulance or paramedics though.' Emma hung her coat on the back of a chair and sat down.

'It's probably round the back to keep it away from the kids,' Dan said, pushing the glass of red wine towards her. She took a gulp. She looked from him to Ed.

'I can't believe what I've just seen,' she said, putting her glass down on the table. 'Was Santa really just found dead in his grotto?'

Dan shook his head in disbelief. 'If I hadn't just seen that with my own eyes, I'd have said you were crazy.'

'The duty news editor thought I was kidding when I filed my copy,' Emma said, indicating outside where she had been pacing. She took another big mouthful from her wine glass.

'Why are the police interviews taking so long?' Ed asked, looking at his phone again.

'Like I said, there's a lot of people around, mate,' Dan said. 'She'll come over as soon as she's finished.'

'She found the body so it stands to reason they'll want to interview her,' Emma said, fiddling with the stem of her glass. 'She was backstage as well; she might have seen something.'

'The Santa guy is the one who's been giving her headaches, isn't he?' Dan said, sipping his pint and looking at Ed.

Ed nodded. 'He's been really messing them around, turning up late and nearly missing the visit to the children's ward at the hospital entirely.'

Emma opened her mouth but, before she could speak, there was a gust of cold air and the man and his friends near the door began to chant 'wood, hole, wood, hole' as if they were cheering for a football team. Their voices died away when they saw Lydia's tear-stained face.

She arrived at the table, pink-cheeked, her usually immaculate French plait looking dishevelled. Dan and Ed got to their feet, the former pointing to the bar.

'A large Highland Park, neat,' Lydia said, answering the question before he asked it. He looked surprised and saluted before disappearing into the crowd.

Lydia took off her coat and hung it on the back of her chair before sitting down. Ed sat down next to her.

'Are you OK?' he asked.

Lydia's face crumpled and tears began to run down her face. He put an arm around her and Emma dug into her handbag, handing over a pocket pack of tissues.

Lydia took one and dabbed at her face and hands. 'I had to wash them for ages to get all the blood off.' She sniffed, holding up her left hand and examining it closely. Dan appeared and placed Lydia's whisky in front of her. She'd gulped down half of it before he even sat down. She coughed slightly. 'Thanks, Dan, that's just what I needed.'

'What happened?' Emma asked, leaning her elbows on the table as Dan sat back down and took a drink from his pint.

'They think Adrian was stabbed,' Lydia said, her bottom lip wobbling. Emma was about to say something when Lydia continued, 'I feel awful. I was so horrible to him the last time I spoke to him.' She kept her eyes on her glass, not looking at any of them.

'Backstage before he got into the window?' Emma asked, raising her eyebrows.

Lydia sniffed and shook her head. 'No, it was at lunchtime on the phone, actually. I didn't see him before he got in the window.'

'You didn't see him when he arrived this afternoon?' Emma asked, surprised. 'I thought you were backstage?'

Lydia shook her head. 'I was— No, I didn't see anyone there.' She shifted in her seat, not meeting Emma's eye.

Emma sipped her drink, watching as Lydia spoke in a low voice to Ed and he hugged her with the arm that was already around her and kissed her softly on the cheek. Lydia was clearly lying. Either she'd seen someone and was protecting them, or she'd already had blood on her hands before she found the body.

Chapter three

'You still haven't confirmed that it's Adrian Kendall?' Emma asked the police press officer in amazement on Monday morning. 'You've had all weekend. What about the people he worked with? Couldn't they do it?'

'My understanding is that it's not been done officially and we haven't informed his family,' the police press officer said. 'They get told first; you know the score.'

'You're telling me that I can't even report that he's been named locally?'

The press officer sighed. 'I'm not telling you, I'm asking you not to. How would you feel if you found out a relative had died through the newspaper and not in person?'

Emma sighed. 'Fair enough. I won't be able to hold my news editor off for long. She's already demanding to know why the name isn't out there. You *can* confirm that Adrian Kendall was stabbed though, right?'

There was a silence at the other end of the phone. 'Who told you that?' the press officer asked, cautiously.

'I know the woman who found him,' Emma said. 'She's my

mate's girlfriend.'

The press officer sighed. 'I thought they'd all been warned not to give interviews to the media.'

'It wasn't an interview. We just met in the pub afterwards.'

'You can't use that, it's not official,' the press officer said quickly. 'I think the post-mortem is today so I'll push the investigating officer for a statement later. I can't guarantee, but I'll do my best.'

Emma thanked her and hung up the phone. She leaned her elbows on her desk and cradled her face in her hands.

'No update?' Dan asked from his desk alongside hers.

Emma sighed. 'They've not even officially ID'd him yet. It sounds like his family is proving hard to find.'

'Couldn't the store manager do it?' Dan asked, swinging his swivel chair to face her.

'The press officer said they're going to do that today and she'll get me an update later. But it could be *hours* before we know anything else.' She picked up her pen and began to tap it rapidly against her desk.

One of the junior reporters popped up from behind her computer, meerkat-style, and glared.

Emma didn't look at her but stopped tapping. 'I still can't believe he was just dead like that,' she said, looking at Dan.

'I know, and poor Lydia found him.'

'Do you think she really didn't see anything?' Emma asked, chewing the end of her pen.

'Because Ed said he left her backstage, do you mean?' Dan asked.

'I was in the shop a couple of days ago and the backstage area looks quite small. How did she miss Adrian coming in to get changed? She *must* have seen him.'

'You think she's lying?' Dan asked, frowning.

'She's hiding something.' Emma scooted her chair over and leaned towards him, lowering her voice. 'She was running the event; he would have had to check in with her when he arrived, surely.' When Dan didn't respond, Emma sat back in her chair. 'What?' she asked, irritated.

'I know you don't like Lydia, but do you really think she'd murder someone?'

Emma glared at him, got to her feet and pulled on her coat.

'Where are you going?' Dan asked, watching her.

'I'm going back to the scene of the crime to see if there were any witnesses who saw Santa before he got into the window. Or saw anyone else loitering about.' She turned away and took two steps, then turned back. 'It's not about me not liking Lydia; Santa didn't stab himself. It has to be someone who was backstage and she was the only one.'

***

The cold wind out in the street stung Emma's face. It whistled through the alleyway at the side of Fenleys as she passed, and a pile of cigarette ends inside the alley told her that she'd found the local smokers' haunt. Sadly there were no handy potential witnesses there today. A cloud of warm air hit her in the face as the department store's automatic doors slid open and she stepped inside.

The curtains remained closed, hiding the display from the shoppers in the street. It also concealed the crime scene investigators who she knew would be crawling all over the grotto. Evergreen garlands had been replaced with blue-and-white police tape. The curtained backstage area was also cordoned off and darkened forlorn Christmas trees stood in a line like guardians, their tinsel drooping as if in mourning. CSIs crawled between and under them. Elsewhere in the shop it was Christmas as usual. Fairy lights flashed and baubles glittered in all directions.

'The police are still hard at work,' Emma remarked to a woman in a Fenleys uniform who was re-stacking a pile of Toblerones.

'Apparently it's the fake snow that's causing a problem,' the woman responded, turning immediately from what she was doing. 'They've been crawling about in there since Saturday.' She glanced over her shoulder and then leaned in towards Emma, who also leaned in. 'You know what happened here, don't you?'

'I heard that the man who plays Santa was taken ill and collapsed,' Emma lied. 'Is he OK?'

The woman shook her head. 'No, dearie, he was murdered. Stabbed in the back.'

Emma faked a gasp. 'Really?'

The woman nodded, pointing to the window area. 'He was right in there, when the curtains opened. Our head of publicity found him.'

'Who would want to stab Santa?' Emma asked, shaking her head in disbelief.

The woman nodded in agreement. 'That's exactly what I said. He's a lovely man, great with the kiddies. I dread to think how they're feeling today. I mean—'

'Reenie?' a voice called.

Emma cursed inwardly. She'd been hoping to keep Reenie going until she told her something she didn't already know. She turned and saw a man in a suit approaching. He was in his mid-thirties, with slicked back dark hair and a smile of incredibly white teeth.

'Those chocolates won't stack themselves,' he told Reenie, 'and I'm sure this young lady has shopping to do.' He smiled at Emma, and Reenie obediently turned back to the table of Toblerones.

'Actually,' Emma said, pointing to his name badge, which said Tony Cootes, Store Manager, 'I was hoping to speak to you about what happened at the opening event on Saturday.'

Tony Cootes's smile disappeared immediately. 'I'm sorry, were you outside? Were your children upset?'

Emma nodded. 'No ... well, yes, I was outside, but I don't have any children.'

Tony Cootes's shoulders relaxed. 'All those poor children, I feel terrible. I can't think what to do to make it up to them.'

Emma nodded. 'I can understand that. I've heard that your Santa was really popular.'

'Yes, the children loved him—' Tony Cootes stopped speaking and Emma hesitated, waiting for him to say how much everyone else liked him too. The words didn't come.

Emma opened her mouth to speak, but a voice cut across her.

'Emma? What are you doing here?' Lydia had appeared silently at her elbow, making Emma jump.

'You two know each other?' Tony Cootes asked, his smile now looking slightly forced.

'This is Emma,' Lydia said, glaring at her. 'She's a reporter at the *Allensbury Post*.'

Tony Cootes's face fell. 'You can't report ... I didn't know that,' he stuttered.

Emma frowned, intrigued by his reaction. 'You haven't said anything.'

Tony Cootes was backing away, his smile now gone. His

mouth opened and shut a few times, then he turned abruptly and hurried away, swerving through the tables piled with mini gumball dispensers, bags of Christmas-scented potpourri and other tat to which Emma would never have given house room. The spaces between the tables weren't wide and he soon collided with a pile of Christmas tea towels. They fell to the floor but he didn't stop to pick them up. Instead, another Fenleys employee had to refold them and return them to the table. Emma had started to follow him, when Lydia grabbed her arm.

'What are you doing here?' Lydia demanded.

Emma shook off Lydia's hand. 'I'm doing my job and collecting information for a story,' she said.

'You should have come to me. I'm the head of publicity,' Lydia snapped, hands on hips. 'You can't just wander around harassing our customers and gossiping.'

'I'm not harassing customers or looking for salacious details—'

'Oh, really?' Lydia's voice was dripping with disdain.

'Yes. Lydia, hundreds of people saw you find Santa dead in his grotto on Saturday night. They deserve to know what happened.' Emma only realised how loudly she was speaking when people started to look at them.

'Lower your voice,' Lydia snapped. 'You're making a scene.'

Emma rolled her eyes. 'Don't speak to me like I'm your servant. I'm doing my job, trying to find out the story so people know what happened and why he died. For some reason you want to stop me. I wonder why that might be?' she asked, tilting her head to the left.

Lydia stepped back as if Emma had slapped her. 'What do you mean by that?' she demanded, hands on hips.

'You're holding something back,' Emma replied, leaning forwards. 'In the pub you said you hadn't seen him backstage, but how could you not? I mean—'

Before she got any further, a woman screamed loudly.

Lydia whipped around. 'That sounded like it came from homewares,' she exclaimed. She turned and ran across the shop floor, Emma in hot pursuit. They arrived at the same time as a security guard.

'There,' he said, pointing at a young woman, with her hands to her mouth, whimpering.

Lydia stopped at the end of the aisle. 'Lotte? What's going on? What's wrong?'

Emma pushed past Lydia and marched over to the woman. She looked at the tray of knives the woman had been tidying. One knife had some red sticky stuff smeared along its eight-inch serrated blade.

'Well done,' Emma said, putting an arm around the woman and pulling her away to a safe distance as the security guard grabbed his mobile from the clip on his belt and began to jab a chubby finger at the screen. 'I think you've just found the murder weapon.'

Chapter four

Once Emma and Lydia had given statements to the police about the finding of the knife, they found themselves pushed back to the blue-and-white police tape, which now cordoned off the homewares area. Tony Cootes stood nearby, alternately wringing his hands and shooing away shoppers who had stopped to gawp.

A couple of detectives were speaking to Lotte Clarke but Emma was too far away to hear what was being said. Lotte had her arms wrapped around her thin torso and when she raised a hand to push a strand of blonde hair behind her ear, Emma could see her hand was shaking. The man was doing most of the talking while the woman scribbled notes.

Suddenly a short, round woman came rushing across the shop, dark hair flying. She resembled a bowling ball so much that Emma thought that if she tripped over she would roll right past them.

'Where is she? Where's my girl?' the woman demanded of no one in particular.

'Hi, Helena,' Lydia said, stepping forward briskly to halt the woman's progress, 'she's over there. She's speaking with the police. If you just—'

Helena gasped and almost elbowed Lydia out of the way. Ignoring the police officer who tried to stop her, she ducked under the tape and dashed down the aisle, dragging Lotte into her arms and almost crushing her in a hug.

'Lotte's mum,' Lydia said quietly to Emma, crossing her arms and leaning against a pillar, which supported the ceiling. 'The floor show is about to start.'

'How did she know this was happening?' Emma asked in a low voice.

'She's probably been standing outside the store watching Lotte through the window,' Lydia replied, puffing out her cheeks.

Emma said nothing, waiting to see what happened.

'What are you doing to my girl? Hasn't she been through enough already?' Helena demanded. Without letting go of Lotte, whose protesting face was pressed so far into Helena's shoulder that Emma was concerned she'd suffocate, she made a sweeping motion with her forearm as if to push the detectives away.

'Please, madam, we need to speak to your daughter to take an initial statement so we can—' the male officer began. He didn't get to finish his sentence. Helena had taken a step forward with her arm still raised defensively. Emma held her breath. 'Madam, please—' he tried again; this time Helena physically pushed him away.

'No, no,' she said. 'My Lotte was so upset by you yesterday that I'm not having it again. I'm taking her home.' She finished with a final jut of the chin as if that closed the matter. She had reckoned without Lotte.

The younger woman disentangled herself from her mother's grasp and moved half a step away. 'Mum, I'm fine. I need to do this now. It's important that—'

Helena was shaking her head and pulling Lotte by the arm down the aisle towards where Emma and Lydia were standing. 'No, this is all too much for you, my darling. I don't think you should work here anymore.'

But Lotte, it seemed, was determined to get her way. She gently freed herself from the hand gripping her arm. 'Mum, I need to do this now and then get back to work,' she said, as if quietening a frightened child. Helena stepped back as if she'd been slapped. 'Seriously, it's OK.' Lotte reached out her hand and patted her mother's arm. 'Go to the store café and I'll buy you a coffee when I'm done here.' She looked at Tony Cootes, who gave her a short nod of agreement. Lotte gestured towards the detectives who were loitering in the background. 'Don't worry, I'll only be a few minutes.'

Helena seemed diminished, as if her daughter's strength had taken the wind from her sails. 'No, I don't want to be in your way,' she said in an aggrieved tone. 'I've only come to support you, and this is the thanks I get.'

'What are you doing here anyway, Mum?' Lotte asked.

Helena glared at her. 'Someone came in the shop and said they'd seen the police here and that you were crying. So I came to help, but if I'm not wanted...' Helena turned and was striding off across the store, back the way she'd come.

Lotte's shoulders slumped and she sighed heavily. Then she straightened the green shirt of her Fenleys uniform, turned and headed back to the police officers.

Emma looked at Lydia. 'That was a scene.'

Lydia pulled a face. 'That's Helena. Always fond of a bit of drama. You should have seen how she behaved on Saturday. I thought she was going to explode at the idea of "her Lotte" being put through all this. As if Lotte's a baby.'

'How old is she?' Emma asked.

'About twenty, I think. Easily old enough to look after herself. Clearly doesn't like her mother's histrionics, but what can she do?' Lydia sighed. 'I feel sorry for her. Imagine having to put up with that every day. And Lotte is so normal. I don't know how she tolerates it.'

Then Lydia seemed to recollect who she was talking to and pulled herself together. 'Well, you'll want to be getting on,' she said to Emma, suddenly all business-like. 'I'm sure the police will give you an update when they've finished here.' She moved in front of Emma, blocking her view of Lotte and the scene. Emma was about to argue but knew she wasn't going to get anywhere for now. She didn't know either of the detectives so she couldn't claim friendship.

She sighed, said goodbye to Lydia and turned to walk away. First the body and now the murder weapon had been found in Fenleys. Why not take the murder weapon away? Unless the killer couldn't risk being caught carrying it. She looked back and saw Lydia watching the CSI who held the knife in a clear plastic tube. Emma was surprised by the expression on Lydia's face. Lotte's discovery of the murder weapon hidden in plain sight was a shock, but instead Lydia looked worried. Very worried.

Chapter five

As Emma left Fenleys, she was accosted by a woman in the smokers' alley. The woman was dragging on a cigarette as if her life depended on it – which Emma found to be a little ironic. She made an effort not to blow smoke in Emma's face, but was only partly successful.

'What's going on in there?' she asked, nodding her head in the direction of Fenleys. She pointed towards the police cars. 'I saw those guys arrive so I thought I'd come out to take a look.'

Emma looked back over her shoulder towards the shop. 'One of the knives in the homewares department has been found with blood on it,' she said. 'They think that—'

'Santa was murdered?' the woman interrupted, wide-eyed. The hand holding the cigarette shook.

Emma nodded. 'It's not official yet. It does look like murder though.' She pointed towards Fenleys. 'Do you work in there?' she asked, although she thought she already knew the answer.

The woman shook her head. 'I don't think I'm their sort of person, do you?' Emma had to admit the woman's cropped turquoise hair and the tattoos poking out of the sleeves and neckline of her t-shirt wouldn't be Tony Cootes's cup of tea. He seemed to prefer them poised, glamorous and well-behaved, like Lydia.

The woman was shaking her head. 'No, I work in there.' She pointed to the Italian café over the road. She puffed out smoke again.

Emma nodded. 'Were you out here yesterday? When the curtains opened?'

The woman nodded. 'I was in the crowd with my little boy and my niece. Say what you like about Fenleys, their Christmas stuff is fab. Proper fake snow and a Santa who really looks like Santa.' She frowned. 'I had to tell the kids that Santa was just poorly or they'd have been devastated. They've made him get well soon cards,' she said, her face softening with pride at their kindness. Taking another drag on her cigarette, she said, 'He was a nice guy.'

'Did you see him out here?' Emma asked, leaning against the wall and then wishing she hadn't when a piece of chewing gum on the wall stuck to the sleeve of her coat.

'He used to stop off and say hi if I was out here. I never saw him smoking though,' the woman said. She smiled. 'He always used to ask if I'd been naughty or nice and then laugh cos I always said naughty. Then he'd say I'd get some coal in my stocking. I told him that wouldn't be very comfortable and it made him laugh even more.' She smiled at the memory. Then she became serious. 'I did see him having a hell of a row with one of the women from there earlier in the week though.' She gestured towards Fenleys with her cigarette.

Emma straightened up. 'What were they arguing about?'

The woman screwed up her face with the effort of remembering. 'I think she said he'd better sort himself out because he was messing things up for everyone else. Said if he didn't, she'd get him fired. She said it wasn't too late to do that.'

Emma leaned forward slightly. 'What did he say?'

'He said there was some personal business that he needed to deal with. When she started to say that wasn't her problem, he said he knew what she'd been up to and if she did anything to him, he'd tell everyone what she'd done. She didn't like that one little bit.'

'What did she say?' Emma asked.

The woman sucked on her cigarette and blew out smoke. 'She said if he tried that, she'd kill him.' Emma raised an eyebrow. 'I know sometimes people can be a bit dramatic,' the woman continued, 'but if you'd seen her face … She did look ready to kill him.'

'What did she look like?' Emma asked.

'Medium height, blonde hair all tied up in a fancy plait, pretty if you like that prissy over-made up look.'

Emma's hands were shaking slightly as she pulled out her phone and opened the gallery of photographs. She selected the one she was looking for and held out her phone to the woman. 'Is that her?'

The woman peered at the screen and then nodded. 'Yeah, that's her.'

Emma looked down at the photograph of Ed and Lydia on her phone, a cold feeling in her stomach. It couldn't have been controlled, buttoned-up Lydia making threats, surely? And what could Lydia possibly have done that would warrant blackmail?

Chapter six

The smoking woman stubbed out her cigarette and, with a wave, headed back to the café. Emma turned in the direction of the newspaper office. She hadn't gone two steps before someone grabbed the back of her coat and pulled her into the alley. Recovering from the shock, she shook herself free and whipped around, ready to defend herself. Tony Cootes cringed away, as if expecting an assault from her clenched fists.

She breathed a heavy sigh of relief. 'It's only you,' she said. 'I thought you were a mugger or something.'

Tony Cootes gave a shaky laugh. 'I'm sorry, I had to stop you.'

'I didn't think you wanted to talk to me,' Emma said, straightening her coat.

'I need to tell you something,' he said, 'but I didn't want anyone to see us.'

Emma stood looking at him, phone still in hand, waiting to hear what he had to say.

Tony Cootes stood there for a moment, rubbing his hands to warm them. It was too cold really to be standing outside in just a suit, shirt and tie.

'Well?' Emma asked. 'What do you want to tell me?'

'I think Lydia might have done something to Adrian,' he said. Emma stared at him. 'What makes you say that?' she asked.

'She's been really angry with him. She kept asking me to fire him and when I said we couldn't do that so close to Christmas, she said she'd take matters into her own hands.'

'Have you told the police this?' Emma asked. When Tony Cootes shook his head, she added, 'I think you should be telling them, not me.'

Tony looked uncomfortable. 'I like Lydia, I don't want to get her into trouble...' He trailed off.

'You think Lydia stabbed Adrian Kendall?' Emma demanded.

Tony Cootes took a step backwards. 'I don't want to think it, but I left her alone backstage. There were hardly any shoppers in the store because they were all outside for the opening. Then I realised I'd left my phone and ducked back inside to get it.'

'And?' Emma demanded, wishing he would get to the point.

'I heard her talking to someone. I wasn't eavesdropping or anything,' he said quickly.

'What did she say?'

Tony Cootes cleared his throat. 'She said something like "no one can ever know what I've done" and then something about a secret.'

'Who was she talking to?' Emma asked, feeling her stomach sink. More evidence that Lydia was lying.

'I don't know, I didn't hear. The countdown was ready to start so I needed to be out front.'

'Do you think she was talking to Adrian?'

Tony Cootes rubbed his arms with his hands. 'He would have been in the backstage area by then.'

'And you think Lydia killed him because of a secret?'

The store manager shrugged. 'Who else was back there apart from them?' he asked.

***

Dan was peering at the screen of his phone and frowning when Emma joined him in the car park behind the *Post*'s building. His face brightened when he saw the takeaway coffees in her hands.

'Latte with a shot of vanilla,' she said, holding out a cup to him.

Dan took it, licking his lips. Then he saw the expression on her face.

'What's the matter?' he asked, peering at her. 'And why the cloak-and-dagger meeting in the car park?'

Emma grabbed his arm and tugged him behind a tree so they couldn't be seen from the office windows.

'Oh, a romantic assignation, is it?' Dan asked, sliding an arm around her and kissing her. Thoughts of Lydia disappeared from Emma's head. Then she broke away. 'You're not getting away that easily,' he murmured into her ear.

'Dan, something important has come up.'

He looked down into her face. 'More important than *this*?' he asked, wiggling his eyebrows.

'Hmmm, now you mention it,' Emma said, leaning in for another kiss.

This time it was Dan who pulled away. 'As this tree doesn't really provide enough coverage for an outdoor quickie – and it's a bit chilly for that kind of behaviour—'

'Is it?' Emma asked, arching an eyebrow and grinning at him. She raised her coffee cup to her lips and pretended to drink innocently.

Dan looked over each shoulder as if checking for eavesdroppers. 'Hmmm, I had no idea that was your kind of thing, Ms Fletcher,' he said, grinning. Then he glanced at his watch. 'Sadly not enough time to discuss it now.'

'Have you got a job to get to?' Emma asked, fiddling with the plastic lid on her coffee cup.

'I need to file some copy from the job I've just been on,' he began, then took in the expression on her face. 'Then again, you look like whatever you're about to say is serious so that can wait. What's up?'

'Is Ed up there?' Emma hissed, pointing at the first-floor office windows.

'Yes,' Dan answered, without lowering his voice. 'Why are you whispering? What's going on?'

'When I was at Fenleys just now, they found the murder weapon.'

Dan's eyes widened. 'What? Where was it?'

'It was in the knife display in the homewares area so it obviously could have been taken from there and then put back after it was used.'

Dan raised the coffee cup to his lips, then seemed to think that it was still too hot and took it away again. 'The killer just put it back?' he asked, frowning.

Emma nodded. 'That means that anyone who works in the shop had access to it.'

'Equally, so could anyone shopping there,' Dan pointed out.

'Only staff would be back there once the window opening happened and the police cordoned off the shop,' Emma said, gesturing at him with her coffee cup.

Dan frowned. 'What are you getting at?'

Emma stepped away, her back turned to him. 'Lydia was backstage,' she said awkwardly, putting her coffee cup to her lips and chewing the plastic lid rather than taking a sip. She scraped the toe of her shoe on the ground, reluctant to say what was going around in her head. When she turned back, Dan was looking at her expectantly. Emma took a deep breath and exhaled heavily. 'She could have put the knife back in the display before the countdown finished,' she said quietly, bracing herself for his reaction.

Dan snorted. 'You mean that she stabbed someone, calmly walked across the shop, ditched the knife and got backstage without anyone noticing her?' He frowned when Emma didn't leap to Lydia's defence. 'Are you serious? You really think that Lydia stabbed Santa?'

'Hear me out,' Emma said, holding up her free hand like someone trying to stop the traffic. She told him about the conversations with the smoking woman and Tony Cootes. 'I told you she's hiding something.'

'And you think it's serious enough that she'd kill someone to keep it quiet?'

'Dan, I don't know what to think.' Emma puffed out her cheeks. 'All I know is that she had the means and opportunity to do it and now it looks like she had a motive as well.'

'What are you going to do about it?'

Emma sighed heavily. 'The only thing I can do: I need to talk to Lydia.'

Dan, who was in the act of taking a sip of coffee, choked. 'You're just going to ask her outright if she killed Adrian?' he demanded between coughs.

Emma glared at him. 'No, but there are so many loose ends. She says she was backstage then claims not to have seen him or anyone else around. How is that even possible?'

Dan took a deep breath. 'I agree it's a bit suspicious,' he said. 'Don't start chucking accusations around without any proof though. I still have to live with Ed and you have to work with him.'

He turned to walk towards the office building and then turned back and held out a hand to her. As she took it, a flash of inspiration told her exactly how to start the conversation with Lydia.

Chapter seven

'This is such a mistake,' Dan said as he stood in the doorway of Emma's kitchen that evening, watching her poke a knife into the lasagne she'd slid out of the oven. 'You can't just trick them into coming round for dinner so you can interrogate Lydia.'

'I'm not planning to interrogate her,' Emma said, satisfied that the lasagne was cooking and sliding it back into the oven.

'Are you going to accuse her of murder?' Dan asked.

Emma turned towards him, a glass of red wine in her hand, and scowled. 'No, I just want to find out what she knows. I told you, she's hiding something.'

Dan walked through to the living room and perched on the sofa. Emma followed, put her glass down on the coffee table and snuggled into him.

He elbowed her gently. 'Don't be trying that to get around me,' he said, moving to put an arm around her. She leaned up and kissed him. 'Hmmm, I can sense myself coming around to the idea,' he said. Emma kissed him again and then sat back to see his reaction. Dan frowned slightly. 'I think I can get on board with this idea,' he said, grabbing her in a bear hug for a long, slow kiss.

The loud chime of the doorbell made them jump apart.

'They'll know something is going on,' Dan said, jumping to his feet. 'We never have them round for dinner on a Monday night.'

'They won't. They'll just think we're being nice,' Emma responded, running her hands through her hair and checking her appearance in the mirror that hung over the mantelpiece.

She went into the hall and opened the door to find Lydia and Ed on the doorstep, both looking slightly apprehensive.

'Thanks for inviting us,' Lydia said, handing over a bottle of red wine as Emma stood back to let them inside. 'It's very kind of you.' Lydia didn't really look like she thought anything of the sort.

'I just thought as you've had such a rough weekend, you might appreciate dinner being cooked for you,' Emma said, her voice sounding false even to herself. She glanced at the label on the bottle of wine and raised her eyebrows at Lydia who smiled.

'Mum and Dad brought it last time they came for dinner. It's a good one, I think. Dad's very into his wine.'

Emma waved them towards the sofa and they both agreed to a glass of wine. Emma disappeared into the kitchen to check on the dinner, leaving Dan to fill up the glasses.

Lydia sat down, looking tired.

Ed was giving Dan a suspicious stare. 'You never ask us round at such short notice,' he said.

Dan shrugged. 'What can I say? Emma thought it might be nice for Lydia to have a break.'

Ed frowned at him and then looked around the room. 'I like the decorations,' he said, indicating the limp strand of tinsel that was draped along the mirror on the wall.

Dan laughed. 'Scrooge Fletcher is a minimalist when it comes to Christmas.'

'I heard that,' Emma said as she returned to the living room. 'I'm not a big fan of Christmas,' she said, looking around, 'unlike Daniel the elf over there.' She poked him in the ribs affectionately as she headed back into the kitchen to answer the beeping of the oven timer. They heard her opening and closing the oven door, then she called, 'Dinner's ready.'

As Dan, Lydia and Ed settled themselves at the table, Emma brought in plates.

'Mmm, lasagne, my favourite,' Ed said, still eyeing Emma.

She tried to smile innocently.

When they were all sitting down, Emma picked up her glass. 'Cheers, guys,' she said. There was a slightly awkward pause as everyone clinked their glasses and took a sip. Emma picked up her cutlery and cut into her lasagne, trying to subtly nudge Dan to get him to begin the conversation. But Dan was keeping well clear and instead she had to begin herself.

'How were things at work after I left?' she asked Lydia.

'I think the word is tense,' Lydia said, forking up a mouthful of lasagne.

'I can imagine,' Dan said, sipping from his glass. 'I mean, finding the murder weapon in the shop must have been a bit of a shock.'

'It was poor Lotte I felt for,' Lydia said, putting down her cutlery, 'but she seemed to cope with it all, even with her mother's dramatics.' She looked at Emma. 'Have they told you anything yet?'

Emma shook her head. 'No updates so far. I don't know what they're doing; it never usually takes this long for some results.'

'You said Tony was worried that the police would insist on

closing the whole store, didn't you?' Ed asked Lydia. 'That would be a total nightmare.'

Lydia took a sip of wine, nodding. 'The window display is shut down, as is the Santa's grotto area on the third floor. The rest of the shop is open. They've given permission to reopen homewares once they've cleaned up.'

They were all silent as they ate a few more mouthfuls. Emma chewed slowly and then said, 'I keep thinking of the murder weapon just lying there. I was saying to Dan that the killer must have dumped it because they might get caught.'

'That sounds reasonable,' Lydia said.

'He or she must have just put it back where they got it from,' Emma said lightly, but Lydia had put down her cutlery.

'I told you I didn't see anyone backstage while the window opening was on,' Lydia said, looking uncomfortable.

Emma took a deep breath. 'Apart from you and Adrian Kendall,' she said, staring straight at Lydia.

Ed's cutlery clattered onto his plate. 'What are you getting at?' he demanded.

'I'm just saying that the killer was obviously in the shop just before the opening. They managed to get backstage, stab Adrian Kendall and put the knife back where they got it from,' Emma replied, putting out a hand to pick up her glass.

Lydia stared at her. 'I didn't see anyone hanging around,' she insisted.

'You didn't even see Adrian backstage?' Emma asked.

Lydia's cheeks flushed. 'Actually, no, he was already in the chair in the window display when I caught him up.' She paused, remembering. 'He was slumped in the chair. I thought he was drunk.'

When Emma continued to stare at her without speaking, Lydia tilted her head to one side. 'Are you suggesting' – she pointed at Emma with her knife – 'that *I* murdered Adrian Kendall?'

'I don't see how you could be in that backstage area and not see Adrian at all,' Emma said. 'That space is tiny; there's no way you could have missed him.'

Lydia leapt to her feet, dropping her cutlery and throwing her napkin onto the table.

Ed also stood up, so quickly he made the table rock. Dan grabbed his own glass to steady it. Ed's tipped over and a red stain spread across the white tablecloth.

'Do you really think that Lydia could kill someone?' he demanded, ignoring the spillage.

Emma looked from him to Lydia and back again without speaking.

'I'm not staying here to be accused,' Lydia said, marching out of the room.

Ed stared at Dan and Emma. 'I can't believe you'd do this,' he said. 'I knew it was suspicious that you'd invited us over for dinner. How could you even think that of Lydia?' When Emma opened her mouth to speak, he held up a hand to stop her. 'I don't want to talk to either of you for now. You've really crossed a line.'

He followed Lydia and they heard the front door slam.

Chapter eight

The slam reverberated around the small living room and the draught blew the lone piece of tinsel off the mirror. Dan turned to Emma, a mixture of anger and sadness on his face.

'Well, that was awkward,' he said, hands on hips. Emma said nothing, twisting her mouth to the right as if holding in words. 'What the hell were you thinking?' Dan asked, quietly. Emma would rather he shouted at her. 'There's no way Lydia is a killer.'

She crossed the room and rearranged the tinsel on the mirror. 'Dan, she's hiding *something*. How could she have been backstage and not seen Adrian? She was right there when he died. She either saw something or she's involved,' she said, turning from the mirror and looking him straight in the eye.

'Why? Why would she kill him?'

'I don't know, that's what's so bloody frustrating,' Emma said, walking to the other side of the room. 'Apart from him being late a few times, she doesn't seem to have a motive. Christmas is definitely ruined now.' She rubbed her face with both palms.

'You can't get past the idea that she's lying?' Dan asked, flopping down on the sofa.

'No,' Emma said, looking around the room as if the solution might suddenly slip out from behind the overstuffed bookcases. She fiddled with a stray curly strand of hair. Then she turned back slowly to face Dan.

'Remember my conversation with Tony Cootes? He said he overheard Lydia talking to someone about a secret.'

'You think that was Adrian backstage with her?' Dan asked, sitting forward and resting his elbows on his knees.

Emma nodded. 'What if he knew what that secret was and was threatening to tell someone?'

Dan frowned. 'What could *Lydia* possibly have done that she wouldn't want anyone to find out about? She's so prim I can't believe she's done something dodgy.'

'We also know that she threatened him,' Emma put in, sitting down beside him.

Dan snorted. 'If you're taking that as a genuine threat, then I might have killed hundreds of people.'

'The problem is,' Emma said, picking up a cushion and fiddling with a button attached to it, 'if Tony Cootes tells the police what he overheard, then Lydia could be in a lot of trouble.'

'You think he genuinely thinks Lydia did it?'

Emma shrugged. 'I don't know. The question is, will the police believe him? And if they do, Lydia is going to need a much better story than what she's told us.

Chapter nine

Emma was in the office on Tuesday morning, fingers hammering away at her keyboard, when the door flew open, crashing against the wall. A red-faced Ed was marching down the office towards her.

'What did you do?' he yelled, throwing his bag onto the floor beside her desk.

'What are you talking about? I haven't done anything.' Emma demanded, shocked at the anger in the normally placid Ed. 'What's going on?'

'What did you tell them?' Ed was shouting so loudly that the whole newsroom had fallen silent.

Emma stood up. 'Don't you dare yell at me,' she shouted back, pointing a finger at him. 'If you told me what the hell you're talking about, then—'

'The police. You told them something, didn't you? Something about the murder?' Ed, hands on hips, was breathing heavily.

Emma stared at him. 'What? No,' she snapped. 'I've not spoken to the police today.'

'Well, thanks to you, Lydia's been arrested.'

Emma stared at him. 'What?' she gasped, feeling her stomach contract.

'The police came to her flat this morning and took her away.'

'And they actually think that—'

Before Emma could say anything else, Dan sauntered into the office with his bag slung across his chest and carrying two takeaway coffee cups. He walked across to Emma.

'Here, I got you this. I know you didn't sleep much last night, but—' He stopped short, suddenly sensing the atmosphere in the office. Emma stood staring at Ed who was still red in the face and breathing heavily. Dan looked at Daisy, the news editor, and at the sub-editors who all stood, some open-mouthed, watching the floor show.

'What's going on?' he asked.

'Lydia's been arrested,' Emma said in a low voice.

Dan stared at her, almost dropping the coffee cups. 'What? When did that happen?' He looked at Ed.

'This morning,' Ed said. 'They came to her flat.' Catching a look between Dan and Emma, he jabbed a finger at her. 'And this is all your fault,' he shouted. 'You've told them something. You've—' He stopped speaking suddenly, his voice breaking.

'Woah, hey, wait a minute,' Dan said, stepping forward and putting the coffee cups down on Emma's desk. 'Emma hasn't told anyone anything.'

'Of course you would say that,' Ed snapped. He snatched his bag off the floor and marched to his desk.

Dan turned and glared at Daisy. She came to life and ordered everyone back to work. With a lot of throat clearing and paper shuffling, they returned to their desks but the junior reporters stood in a group whispering, eyes locked on the senior reporters as they gathered around Ed's desk.

'Emma didn't tell the police anything,' Dan said, walking over and sitting down in the empty chair next to Ed. 'I was with her all evening and night and she didn't call anyone.'

Ed glared at Emma as she followed Dan. He stood up suddenly, making her take a step backwards, and Dan waved for him to let Emma join them. When Ed sat back down, she perched on the low filing cabinet next to his desk.

'What actually happened? What did they say?' he asked Ed.

'We were at Lydia's place getting ready for work and there was a knock at the door. It was two police officers and they said she had to go with them for questioning.'

'They didn't officially arrest her?' Dan asked.

'Well, not in so many words but you could see they were going to. It's usually the next step, isn't it?' Ed was glaring at Emma.

She shook her head. 'Not necessarily. They—' She stopped short when Ed growled at her.

'Look, Emma's got nothing to do with it,' Dan said.

Ed got to his feet suddenly, making both Dan and Emma start backwards. 'I can't stay here. I've got to go to the cop shop and find out what's going on.' He grabbed his bag and stormed out of the room.

Daisy called to him, asking where he was going but he ignored her.

Emma put her face in her hands. 'Tony Cootes,' she said, between her fingers.

Dan nodded, getting up and walking back to his desk, picking up his coffee cup as he passed Emma's. 'We saw this coming,' he said, sitting down to switch on his computer, 'and, like you said, Lydia better have a story worked out.'

Emma returned to her desk and sat down, resting her elbows on her desk.

Dan was looking at her. 'What are you going to do?' he asked in a low voice.

'Lydia is hiding something, there's no doubt. I need to find out who else would have wanted to kill Adrian Kendall. All we know about him is that he was a nice man who played Santa, so why would someone murder him?'

'You mean *he* might have been into something dodgy?'

Emma nodded. 'And if there was someone else backstage stabbing Adrian, they might now be worried that Lydia saw something. If she's not the killer, she could be the next victim and I'm not having that. Proving who really did it could be the only way to save her.'

***

With Dan dispatched to cover the proceedings in Allensbury Magistrates' Court for the morning, Emma settled down to investigate. The coffee he'd bought for her was microwaved by one of the juniors on a tea run and the caffeine was soon helping her brain to fire up.

'There's only a few reasons people commit murder,' she'd said to Dan before he left.

'Greed, anger and jealousy?' he'd asked.

She'd nodded. 'So I need to find someone who knows Adrian who can tell me whether there's anyone who might have felt one of those things about him.'

She was working her way through the electoral roll and squinting at the screen of her computer. She found Adrian easily and made a note of his address in case it came in useful. Then she found a couple of other Kendalls. Armed with those details,

Emma decided to get away from the desk and head out to search in person.

She earned a smile from Daisy when she said she was on the trail of a family member. As she left the office, Emma made a promise to herself: she wouldn't stop until she found out who killed Adrian Kendall. She just hoped it wasn't going to cost her Ed's friendship if it turned out to be Lydia.

Chapter ten

The daytime traffic in Allensbury was light and it didn't take Emma long to find two of the addresses and establish that those Kendalls didn't know Adrian. Ten minutes later she reached the address she had for a Martin Kendall. Carefully parking in a space at the end of the cul-de-sac facing towards the main road, she grabbed her handbag and climbed out of the car.

'Eighteen, nineteen, twenty,' she muttered under her breath as she located the large house, set back a little way from the road. The drive was paved in red bricks, identical to its neighbours, and there were no weeds growing between the stones. The lawn was meticulously mowed and the flowerbed was planted with rose bushes, which were neatly pruned for the winter months.

She reached the door and pressed the doorbell. It rang but there was no accompanying movement to suggest that someone was coming to answer the door. After waiting about a minute, Emma pushed the doorbell again. There was no response.

She contemplated leaving a message asking him to call her, then decided it was better to leave it open for her to call again. She had no idea if this was the right Kendall.

She was walking back down the drive when a woman wearing a Barbour body warmer and gardening gloves popped up from behind the hedge that separated Martin Kendall's property from next door, making her jump.

'What are you doing?' she demanded, in the way of people with money when they encounter someone beneath them.

Emma smiled. 'Hi, I'm looking for Martin Kendall,' she said, pointing back over her shoulder at the house. She felt sure this neighbour was the type to know what was what in the cul-de-sac.

'What do you want with him?' The woman's eyes were narrowed and Emma wondered what button to press to open the gossip floodgates.

'I'm from the *Allensbury Post* circulation department,' she lied. 'Mr Kendall has had problems with his subscription so I thought, as I was in the area, I'd pop by.'

The woman eyed her for a moment, then clearly considered that Emma was being suitably deferential in coming to visit a customer.

'I see,' she said, adjusting the expensive-looking scarf coiled around her neck. Then she frowned. 'I didn't know Martin got a newspaper.'

Emma stifled a grin. Clearly this woman was the nosy neighbour of the street.

'I'd hoped to catch him at home,' she said. 'He must be at work.'

'Actually I've not seen him today,' the neighbour said, distractedly pulling at a leaf that was growing out from the neatly trimmed hedge. 'I see him every morning when he goes out. He usually waves, but I don't remember seeing him.'

Emma frowned. 'Did you see him yesterday?'

The woman thought for a moment. 'Now you mention it,'

she said slowly, 'I don't recall seeing him then either. That is unusual,' she said, pointing the leaf at Emma.

'Maybe he's away on holiday,' Emma said, smiling. She shook her head. 'I really should have checked whether he had a hold on his subscription before I left the office.' Despite her winter coat she could feel her teeth beginning to chatter and glanced at her watch. 'I should get back.'

She thanked the woman and turned to go, then turned back. 'Does Mr Kendall live alone?' she asked.

The neighbour looked surprised. 'Yes, ever since his divorce. He was lucky to keep the house,' she said in a slightly gossipy tone.

Normally Emma would have let this kind of chat run on, but she was playing out a theory in her head. 'Ah, that makes sense. I had another Kendall on my list to speak to about a subscription. Obviously it wouldn't be the same house, would it?' She gave a little laugh as if at her own silliness. 'I don't suppose he has a brother?'

'Him,' the neighbour said scornfully. 'He was a brother in name only.'

Emma could feel her pulse quicken. 'Did he come round a lot?' she asked.

'Not really, although every time he did, there was a row over something or other.' She paused. 'We could hear them shouting from next door,' the woman said, pointing her thumb back at her own house.

'When was Mr Kendall's brother last here?' Emma asked.

The neighbour thought for a moment. 'It was Friday, I think. I heard raised voices again as usual, they didn't seem angry though. More excited. Well, Adrian sounded excited, Martin seemed to be trying to calm him down. I heard him say, "I'll do anything to help, anything, you know that." Adrian said, "I don't like to ask, but I may have no choice. We have to get her out of there." Then Martin said, "Think about what you're doing. Don't you think she's been hurt enough?"' She paused.

'And then what happened?' Emma asked.

'Then my husband turned the TV up and I couldn't hear any more,' the neighbour finished regretfully.

Emma frowned, trying to process the information. She looked up to see the neighbour staring at her. 'Well, thank you for your time,' Emma said, looking down at her watch. 'I need to get back to the office now. I'll pop by later to see if Mr Kendall is home.'

She turned away and the neighbour looked disappointed. Emma walked to her car, mind whirling. She definitely needed to find Martin Kendall and hope she found him in a chatty mood.

Chapter eleven

When Emma got back to the office, she found Dan back at his desk tapping rapidly at his computer keyboard.

He glanced up and smiled. 'Hey, babes, how goes it?' he asked, with a wink.

Emma laughed. 'I thought we decided against pet names,' she said.

Dan shrugged. 'Maybe you're right, it doesn't suit you. How about snuggle muffin?'

Emma walked over and punched him lightly on the arm. 'I think not,' she said with a grin. 'Certainly not in public.'

'Fair enough,' Dan agreed, turning back to his computer.

'You're finished at court?' Emma asked, taking off her coat and hanging it on the back of her chair. She folded her scarf and laid it on her desk.

'Ed couldn't get anything out of the police so he came to take over from me.'

Emma sat down. 'How's he doing?'

'In shock now,' Dan said. 'Less angry, just can't get his head around it. He's worried about what they're doing to Lydia.'

'They're hardly going to torture her for information,' Emma said, turning to her computer and switching on the monitor. It lit up and she input her password.

'Yeah, you know Lydia. She doesn't exactly come across well on first meeting,' Dan said, turning back to his computer screen but not typing.

Emma nodded. 'If she gives the police the dismissive act, they're not going to like it.'

Dan sighed and nodded. 'She can be her own worst enemy,' he said.

Emma looked at him, hands poised over the keyboard. 'If the police get the idea that she's lying about something...' She trailed off.

'They'll think she murdered him?' Dan asked.

Emma sighed. 'Possibly. In other news, I spoke to Adrian's brother's nosy neighbour,' she said.

Dan spun on his chair, knocking his notebook to the floor. 'You found his brother?' he asked, bending down to retrieve it and almost falling off the chair.

Emma nodded. 'He lives in quite a posh bit of town. His neighbour said she overheard Martin a few days ago telling Adrian he'd do anything to help but hadn't he hurt her too much already.'

'Hurt who?'

'She missed that part of the conversation. It sounds like we were right and Adrian was up to something.'

Dan took a deep breath and puffed out his cheeks. 'Something that got him killed?' he asked.

Emma looked at him and scratched her nose. 'Maybe he did hurt that person and they retaliated,' she said.

Dan fiddled with the spiral binding on his notebook. 'Maybe.

Does that sound like it involves Lydia?'

Emma frowned. 'You think that Martin meant Adrian was hurting her by messing up the preparations for opening night?' she asked, looking doubtful.

'Tony Cootes said he overheard Lydia and Adrian talking about a secret. Maybe it was that?'

Emma shook her head. 'Tony said he overheard Lydia talking. He didn't say she was talking *to* Adrian.'

'Fair enough,' Dan said, putting his notebook down on his desk. 'What are you going to do?'

'I need to find out more about our Santa,' she said, 'and why someone wanted him dead.'

Emma's previous research on Adrian Kendall had identified him as an actor with an impressive portfolio of television, theatre and radio credits going back twenty years. The image search showed him as a young man, clearly the heart-throb of the long-running police procedural TV show he'd been starring in.

Daisy, the news editor, walked past behind Emma and wolf-whistled. 'Who is *that*?' she asked.

Emma looked up at her. 'The Santa who just got killed,' she replied.

Daisy frowned and leaned on the back of Emma's chair. 'I thought he was much older than that.'

Emma rolled her eyes and pointed at the screen. 'This was twenty years ago.'

The woman sighed. 'I can't get over the fact that someone killed him,' she said. 'He looks like a nice guy.'

Emma nodded. 'So I've heard from almost everyone I've spoken to,' she said.

Daisy leaned down beside Emma and spoke in a low voice. 'Is there any update on what's happening with Ed's girlfriend?' she asked. 'I daren't ask after his reaction earlier. I can't believe she's been arrested.'

Emma shook her head. 'I've not heard anything from the police, or from Ed.'

'Well, let me know when you do.' Daisy turned and walked back to her desk.

Emma returned to her research and the website of Weldon Actors' Agency, which said it represented Adrian.

Out of the corner of her eye she saw Dan click his mouse once and wave at Daisy. She acknowledged him and he turned to Emma.

'What have you got?' he asked, scooting his chair over to look at her screen.

'Adrian Kendall was an actor, has been for years.' She pointed to the list of credits. 'A successful one at that. He's got a cracking back catalogue. I remember that one from when I was little.' She pointed to a children's drama. 'He played the older brother.'

'He was a good-looking bloke back then,' Dan said, 'if you like that sort of cheesy white smile.'

Emma laughed and pointed to the more recent headshot, which showed Adrian hadn't lost the twinkle in his kind eyes. 'He's still got something about him,' she said. 'That face is too smooth to grow a beard good enough for Santa though. No wonder he has to fake it.'

Dan was silent as he looked at the pictures of Adrian over the years, from West End plays to panto to TV ads.

Then he pointed to the screen. 'Look where he trained: Allensbury Dance and Drama School,' he said.

'So he's a local boy made good,' Emma said. 'It's definitely worth putting a call in to them and seeing what they can tell me.' She made a note of the address of Weldon's. Then, shutting down her computer, she stuffed her notebook into her handbag and checked her watch.

'Right,' she said getting to her feet. 'Time to call on Joe Weldon and see what he can tell me.'

Chapter twelve

A flurry of snow began to fall outside as Emma pushed open the door to Weldon's. The office was on the first floor above a newsagent on the high street. Not a glamorous location, she thought, as she climbed the stairs. Through the door at the top, she found an empty reception room. Truth be told, the room was more desk than anything else. There was just enough space for a couple of chairs for people to wait in. She thought that might not matter if not many people came in. There had been a loud buzz when she'd opened the downstairs door, but it was a minute or two before a man responded. He burst out of a door to the side of the desk, almost colliding with it.

'Hello,' he boomed, his voice also too large for the small room. 'Come in.' He looked Emma up and down. 'Let me guess: actor, looking for work as the patient best friend of the leading lady.' He beamed. 'I'm good at spotting potential.'

Emma smiled back. 'No, I'm a reporter at the *Allensbury Post*,' she said.

The man looked surprised. 'Are you after some review tickets?' he asked.

Emma shook her head. 'No, I wanted to talk to you about Adrian Kendall.'

The man's face fell. 'So sad,' he said. 'This is the first time I've had a client murdered. I've been trying to contact his brother to offer my condolences.' He paused. 'Why do you want to know about Adrian?'

'We're putting together a tribute piece,' Emma said. 'I haven't been able to speak to his family either and I wondered if you'd be able to help.'

'Oh, good. He deserves one. He's well-known in theatre circles. Come through to my office.'

Emma squeezed past the reception desk and followed him through the door at the side into another office, only slightly larger than the reception area.

'My secretary is out on her lunch at the moment,' he said, indicating the desk as Emma squeezed past. 'She asked for a bigger desk and I may have got confused between inches and centimetres when I ordered it.' He winced and Emma smiled. She was warming to Joe Weldon. 'So,' he said, indicating a chair for her and sitting down behind his desk, 'what can I tell you?'

Emma sat down and slipped her notebook and pen out of her handbag. 'How long had Adrian been with you?'

Joe thought for a moment. 'About five or six years? Since he moved back from London anyway.'

'And he was local originally?'

Weldon nodded. 'Yes, I saw him in some productions when he was at college here, many, many years ago. I was pretty new and wanted to build my business up quickly. He was very good and willing to try his hand at all sorts of roles. Yeah, I figured if I could get a couple of strong contenders on my books then I'd attract the notice of production companies.'

'He didn't sign with you?' Emma asked, scribbling in her notebook.

Joe shook his head. 'I got gazumped by one of the big London talent agencies. Well, you know how it goes, they come and watch opening nights at college performances and local theatre. They can almost guarantee roles for an actor straight out of college, or at least that's what they promise.'

'Did that work for Adrian?' Emma asked, pen flying across her notebook as her shorthand battled to keep up with Joe's rapid speech.

'Yes, it did. Not that I was at all surprised. He was a big talent. Could make you believe anything. I'd been in talks with him about signing up but his head was turned by the bright lights.' He shrugged.

'You weren't upset about that?' Emma asked.

Joe shrugged again. 'You win some, you lose some. He was almost apologetic about going elsewhere. I think it was because we stayed on good terms that he contacted me when he was moving back. Wanted to see if he could join my books.'

'Why did he come back?'

'He wasn't getting the work elsewhere anymore. He said that his agent was too focused on the "big names" they had on their books and weren't getting him the jobs he wanted. He was a sensible guy compared to some actors and had made hay while the sun shone.' When Emma looked puzzled, he said, 'Adrian had saved up some money while the going was good, not enough to keep living in London long term though, so he came home.'

'Was he getting work here?'

'He's done more theatre recently, with local companies and playing the panto dame in Tildon for a couple of years. He loved that,' Joe said with a smile. 'He loved anything to do with entertaining kids. I think it's because he never had any of his own.'

'Was he married?'

Joe shook his head. 'Nope, never been married. Big loss, I always thought. He'd have been great at family life.'

Emma came to the end of her scribbling and looked up. 'How did he get the Fenleys gig?'

'I've been providing their Santa for ten years or more, so when they're casting they come straight to me. My usual Santa retired a few years ago and Adrian jumped at the chance to fill the red suit.'

Emma raised an eyebrow. 'Someone who'd been playing to the bright lights in London was happy to be a local Santa?'

Joe smiled. 'That's the thing about Adrian, he never got spoiled by the hype. Some people get big-headed, he just wanted to work. Like I said, he loved entertaining kids.'

'So as usual you got the call from Fenleys this year?'

Joe shook his head. 'No, that's the thing. They didn't call. So I called them.'

'And?'

'They'd already cast another guy in the role.'

'What did Adrian do?'

'He lost it. Completely. I'd never seen him get so much as mildly irritated, even when he'd lost out on parts he really wanted, but he went nuts. Started shouting at me. I told him there was nothing I could do.'

'What did he do next?' Emma asked.

'He stormed out of here, slammed the door like a right prima donna. That wasn't like him at all.'

'Where did he go?'

Joe sighed. 'My guess is that he went to Fenleys and spoke to the manager there because the next day I got a phone call from them saying their Santa arrangement had fallen through and can they have Adrian as usual.'

Emma frowned. 'That's a bit odd,' she said.

'It's not unheard of. I found out who the other guy was and checked in with him. He said he's OK though because he'd managed to get the Santa gig down at Tildon shopping centre. They'd been let down.'

Emma sat back in her chair, thinking hard. When she looked up at Joe, he was looking back at her expectantly.

'Just one more question: who did you speak to at Fenleys?'

'The manager, Tony Cootes. I think he's relatively new there and maybe he wanted to shake things up a bit. Whatever happened, whatever was said, Adrian got the gig.' His mouth turned down at the corners. 'Though I wish he hadn't, given what's happened.'

Emma thanked Joe and headed back outside where the snow continued to swirl in the air. She was putting her notebook away in a daze and almost walked into a man coming in the opposite direction. Tony Cootes hadn't wanted Adrian as the Fenleys' Santa this year. Why was he so against the idea, and, more importantly, who convinced him to change his mind?

***

As Emma walked into the office, she saw Ed sitting at his desk, typing energetically. He glanced up when she arrived at her desk. She braced herself for another argument, but he didn't speak.

'How's Lydia?' she asked tentatively.

'They've let her go, pending further enquiries,' he snapped.

'She's gone back to work.'

'That's good news.'

Ed looked up at her and stopped typing. 'They're still looking for more evidence. They don't have any more questions yet. They were very emphatic about the "yet",' he said, glaring at her.

'Ed, I didn't tell anyone anything,' she said quietly. Ed's eyes were studiously fixed on his screen and he was typing quickly.

Emma opened her mouth to speak, but closed it again when she saw the sticky note on her monitor. It read 'Please call Suzy in the police press office' followed by a number.

Without sitting down, Emma picked up the phone and dialled the number, which she already knew by heart.

When Suzy answered, Emma listened. In fact, her only part in the conversation was to say 'hello', 'Are you kidding me?', 'thank you' and 'goodbye'. Ed looked up at her. Emma stared at him in disbelief.

'What?' he asked.

'I need to speak to Lydia,' she said, grabbing her handbag. 'Now.'

***

Emma nearly flattened several Christmas shoppers as she sprinted up the hill and along the high street to Fenleys. She dashed through the doors of the department store and skidded to a halt, looking around for Lydia. Fortunately she saw a familiar blonde plait standing in the homewares area chatting to Lotte Clarke, who was restocking a shelf of glasses, and hurried across the shop floor.

She called Lydia's name and when Lydia turned and saw her,

she began to walk away.

'Stop, Lydia, stop,' Emma shouted. 'I need to talk to you.'

Lydia turned back and folded her arms as Emma skidded to a halt in front of her. 'Oh, do you? After you told the police I killed Adrian?' she snapped.

'Lydia, I didn't say anything to them,' Emma gasped, trying to catch her breath. She was way too out of condition to be sprinting anywhere. 'I needed to tell you,' she said, grabbing Lydia's arm and dragging her to the side. She bent forward, hands on her knees as she fought to catch her breath. Then she straightened up and looked Lydia in the eyes. 'I had a call from the police. It wasn't Adrian Kendall.'

'What wasn't Adrian?' Lydia asked, staring at Emma.

'Santa ... it wasn't Adrian Kendall. He's not dead.'

Behind Lydia, there was a loud smash as Lotte Clarke knocked over a whole shelf of glasses.

Chapter thirteen

Emma and Lydia both jumped and spun around to stare at Lotte. The younger woman stared at the pile of broken glass at her feet, her hands clasped to her mouth.

'What did you just say?' she whispered, moving towards Emma.

Emma looked from the smashed glass on the floor to Lotte's wide brown eyes. 'I said the police just told me that it wasn't Adrian Kendall in the Santa suit.'

'Who was it?' Lotte asked.

'His brother, Martin,' Emma replied.

'What was his brother doing dressed as Santa?' Lotte asked.

Emma shook her head. 'I've no idea. You didn't see him then?'

Lotte shook her head. 'No, I was, somewhere else. I was...' Her voice trailed away. Then she cleared her throat and looked back at the broken glass. 'I'd better, um, better get something to clear this up.' She gestured towards the mess and then with a flick of long blonde hair, she turned and hurried away across the shop floor towards a door marked 'staff only' before Emma or Lydia could say anything else. They stared at each other as the door slammed behind her.

'What was all that about?' Emma asked.

Lydia shook her head. 'No idea.' Then she frowned. 'I didn't know Adrian had a brother. What was he doing dressed as Santa?'

'Maybe Adrian was running late again or wasn't going to turn up and didn't want you to know,' Emma said, looking at the smashed glass on the floor.

Lydia followed her gaze. 'We'd better wait here until Lotte gets back. I don't want anyone getting hurt.' She frowned and looked across the shop. 'How long does it take to fetch a dustpan? I saw it earlier. It's right next to the door.'

Suddenly the door swung open and Lotte reappeared carrying a dustpan, two brushes and a small plastic bin.

Without meeting Emma or Lydia's eyes, she began to studiously sweep up the glass and brush it into the dustpan.

Emma watched Lydia carefully as the latter moved towards Lotte to steady the dustpan and pour the contents into the bin when it was full.

When Lydia spoke again it was almost to herself. 'I didn't know Martin Kendall,' she said. 'So why would I kill him? The police will have to believe that.' She looked up and caught Emma watching her. 'What?' she demanded.

'Everyone thought it was Adrian,' Emma said. 'To be honest, in the suit and that beard, it could have been anyone.'

Lydia glared at her.

'If you didn't do it, you've got to admit that it's odd that someone was attacked and stabbed and you saw and heard nothing,' she said, watching Lydia closely.

Lydia looked as if she was going to say something but changed her mind. She picked up the second brush and became very interested in sweeping a piece of floor that was already completely clear of glass. Emma watched her for a moment, frowning. Lydia looked up at her and seemed about to speak when a voice rang out.

'Lydia? What are you doing here?' It was Tony Cootes striding towards them. Then he saw what they were doing and his face fell. 'For God's sake, what's gone on here?'

Lydia got to her feet smoothly. 'I think the shelf gave way, Tony,' she said. 'Lotte was stacking the glasses when it just collapsed. I know someone complained that it was loose a couple of days ago. I left you a note,' she said earnestly. A sideways glance to Emma suggested she'd done no such thing.

Not wishing to admit he'd been in the wrong, Tony Cootes blustered. 'Well, I, erm, yes, just get this cleaned up, will you?' he said to Lotte. She nodded without looking up or speaking and Emma noticed her hands were shaking slightly.

Then Tony seemed to think of something. 'When did you get here? I thought you were being interviewed by the police?'

'I was but they've let me go.'

Tony Cootes nodded and cleared his throat a couple of times. He ran a finger around the inside of his collar and then noticed Emma for the first time. 'What are you doing here?' he demanded.

'Emma came to tell me that it wasn't Adrian who got stabbed,' Lydia said.

Tony Cootes's shoulders sagged and he nodded. 'The police told me earlier. They called to ask if I would go to identify the body. I told them I don't know his brother so it wouldn't have been any use.'

'Did he not have any ID on him?' Lydia asked.

Tony nodded. 'His wallet was in his coat pocket. It was hanging up backstage so they took that with them.' He sighed. 'They have to do a face-to-face identification as well, so they're looking for someone who knew Martin.'

'I bet that was a bit of a shock finding out,' Emma said. 'Did you not realise at the time?'

Tony Cootes shook his head awkwardly. 'I was so shocked that I didn't really look at him. Plus with the beard and...' He trailed off.

'You saw Adrian because that's what you were expecting?' Emma asked.

He nodded. Then he seemed to shake himself and decide he'd said enough. 'Lydia, I need to see you in my office. There's things we need to discuss, once you've disposed of that.' He pointed to the glass and then turned on his heel, striding away across the shop floor.

Lydia and Emma stared after him. Lotte swept the last few pieces of glass into the dustpan and stood up.

'Thanks for not dropping me in it,' she said to Lydia.

'Don't worry, your secret is safe,' Lydia said, taking the glass-filled dustpan and emptying it into the bin. 'I'll get rid of this,' she said, pointing at the bin. 'I'll get the cleaner to come and hoover as well.' She waved a hand at the floor. 'Stay here until I get back.' She turned and began to walk away. Emma followed.

'What are you going to do now?' Lydia asked.

'If Adrian Kendall isn't dead, where is he? I need to find him and quickly ... before whoever killed Martin does.'

***

The intervention of Daisy when Emma returned to the office

meant it was after five o'clock as she pulled into a parking space outside Adrian Kendall's flat. Several of his neighbours were returning home from work, a mixture of factory uniforms and young people in business suits, the complete opposite of his brother's very middle-class property. The flat was in a converted post-war detached house, which had been divided into two. The paint on the wooden front door and windows was peeling. Checking the address in her notebook, Emma approached the door numbered 6A. The plastic marker beside the front door bell was so scratched that Emma could barely read the name 'Kendall' beside it. She raised a finger, pushed the doorbell and waited, hearing it ring abruptly inside. She braced herself for whatever reception she got. Nothing happened. She pressed the doorbell again and heard it ring again. This time she saw movement behind the net curtains that hung across the window. Clearly there was someone in there, but the door wasn't opened.

Falling back on the excuse she'd given to Martin Kendall's neighbour, she called, 'Mr Kendall? I'm from the *Allensbury Post*. I wanted to discuss your subscription.' There was still no answer and no more movement behind the curtains. Whoever it was, they weren't going to show themselves now. She dug in her handbag and found a business card. She scribbled a note on the back, asking Adrian to call, and then pushed it through the letterbox.

She walked away down the path, making sure she could be seen by the person inside, and headed back to her car. She pulled out of the parking space and started to drive away, but instinct told her to park further up the road. With her back to the flat, she angled her rear-view mirror so that she could see the door of the flat without turning round, and then she settled down to wait.

Her instinct was rewarded. Ten minutes later the front door

opened. Emma blinked in surprise as Lotte Clarke stepped out and carefully locked the door behind her. She was carrying a heavy-looking holdall and, with a quick glance up and down the street, she turned and walked away quickly.

Chapter fourteen

'Lotte Clarke? The woman from Fenleys? The one who knocked all those glasses over?' Dan paused with a forkful of spaghetti halfway to his mouth. Emma swallowed her mouthful and nodded. They were sitting at the rectangular wooden dining table in Dan and Ed's flat.

'Yup. I could hear there was someone inside,' she said. 'I assumed it was Adrian so I hung around to try to speak to him.'

'Why would she have a key?' Dan asked, before resuming eating.

Emma put down her cutlery and took a sip from her glass of water. She rested her elbows on the table and clasped her hands together.

'I don't know. No one has said anything to me so far about them even knowing each other.'

Dan raised an eyebrow and Emma stopped in the act of winding spaghetti around her fork. 'You think they're a couple?'

'Why else would she have a key to his flat? Plus Santa usually has a Mrs Claus, doesn't he?'

Emma glared as Dan laughed.

'It's a big age gap from your early twenties to mid-forties,' she said.

'Not beyond the realms of possibility though, is it?'

Dan forked down a few mouthfuls while Emma stared off into the distance.

'I keep coming back to the fact that Adrian loved being Santa,' she said.

'So?'

'Well, the window opening ceremony was "the" moment of the Christmas season at Fenleys,' Emma said, sipping water again. 'Lydia said that Adrian had been a bit slapdash, almost missing publicity shots and suchlike, but would he really miss the *opening*? Why would he send his brother in his place for the big night?' She took a mouthful of pasta and chewed slowly.

'Maybe Martin was there in case Adrian was late?' Dan asked. 'At least then there would be a Santa.'

'Why would you risk being late for something so important to you?'

'I think that's the million dollar question, isn't it?' Dan said, watching her closely. 'What's your next move?'

After a few minutes of silent eating, Emma put down her fork. 'Two things. I need to talk to Tony Cootes again. He was backstage around the time Martin was killed. He told the police about overhearing Lydia having a conversation.'

'And?'

'There's no one who can confirm where he actually was or how long he was there for.'

'And the second thing?'

'Lotte Clarke. Where was she when Martin was killed, and why has she got a key to Adrian's flat?'

Chapter fifteen

When Emma walked into the office on Wednesday morning, one of the junior reporters flapped a hand at her to come to his desk. Seeing the sceptical look on her face at being summoned in that way, he pointed at his phone and waved for her to hurry up, almost bouncing in his chair.

Dumping her bag on her desk, Emma crossed the room and took the phone. 'Hello?'

'Is that Emma Fletcher, the one who's written about Martin Kendall's murder?' a posh female voice demanded.

Emma raised her eyebrows. 'Speaking,' she replied, not in the mood for what sounded like it could be a complaint.

'I want to speak to you.'

Emma looked down at the junior. 'Who is it?' she mouthed. He shook his head and shrugged.

'Hello? Are you there?' The shrillness of the voice made Emma jump.

'Yes, sorry, I am. How can I help?'

'You do those nice stories, don't you, about people who've died, asking their friends about them?' the woman gabbled.

'Yes,' Emma said, perching a hip on the desk. The junior reporter grabbed his glass of water before her bulky winter coat could knock it over.

'I want you to do one about Martin,' the woman continued. 'He was a lovely man and a good neighbour; someone should say something nice about him. His good-for-nothing brother certainly won't.' The woman continued speaking rapidly and Emma twigged: this was the nosy neighbour she'd met on Martin's driveway. Perfect.

'Of course, I was hoping to find someone who'd tell me more about him. Do you have a moment now to chat?' Emma prepared to transfer the call to her own phone but the woman interrupted.

'No, I've got a church meeting this morning. Come at one o'clock.'

Remembering that she'd lied about who she was when they'd met, Emma asked for the woman's contact details. She rattled off her address and then hung up without saying goodbye.

Emma nodded thanks at the junior reporter. He looked relieved to have his desk back when she walked away.

When Emma arrived in Martin Kendall's street, she parked at the entrance of the cul-de-sac facing towards the main road and smiled to herself. She doubted that the neighbour posed a threat, but she'd automatically parked for a quick getaway. She walked up the driveway and pressed the bell, seeing a net curtain twitch. The chimes of Big Ben played back at her loudly, making her jump, and the door opened immediately.

The woman stared at her. 'You? I thought you did subscriptions.'

Emma smiled. 'Sorry for the subterfuge,' she said. 'I am actually the crime reporter.'

The woman seemed to consider for a moment, but then waved Emma inside and peered out, as if checking to see if anyone had spotted her visitor. She shepherded Emma into an enormous living room with squashy chintz sofas. Emma sat as directed and almost disappeared into the cushions. No chance of a quick getaway from here, she thought. The neighbour disappeared into the kitchen and returned with a tray of teapot, china cups and saucers, a milk jug and what looked like homemade biscuits.

'I'm glad you've come,' the neighbour said, sitting down and pouring without asking if Emma wanted a drink. Once Emma had milk in her tea and her cup and saucer on a neat side table, the woman introduced herself as Mrs Hurley. 'Martin deserves to have his death marked,' she said. 'He did a lot for charity and he's got no other family to do anything.'

Emma flipped open her notebook and wrote down the word 'charity'. 'What about his brother. Has he not been to the house or contacted you?'

Mrs Hurley snorted. 'He wouldn't think of that. He wouldn't think that Martin and I were friends and that I might want to be of help to him.'

Emma smiled to herself. She had a feeling Martin would not agree that Mrs Hurley was a friend.

'Martin always had a polite word when I saw him,' Mrs Hurley continued.

'Was that often?' Emma asked.

Mrs Hurley sipped delicately from her cup. It was elegantly balanced on the saucer in her hand. 'Oh, every day. I'd see him coming and going from work. He'd always wave and say hello if I was in the garden.'

Emma could imagine Mrs Hurley loitering in the garden every day waiting for Martin to return. 'Do you know where he worked?' she asked, pen poised over her notebook.

'He was an accountant, he worked for a firm in town. Gateby and Sons.'

Emma made a note. 'You mentioned that he did a lot of work for charity,' she said, reaching over carefully to pick up her cup and take a sip.

'He was involved in the local Rotary, of course,' Mrs Hurley said, 'and he also did fun runs and other things like that for a local children's cancer charity. He loved children.'

One thing he had in common with his brother, Emma thought.

'Did he have children?' she asked, looking across at Mrs Hurley.

'No, he and his wife weren't blessed in that direction. Although' – Mrs Hurley leaned forwards as if telling a state secret – 'I think he would have loved them, but she refused. A career woman, you see.' She pursed her lips and gave a disapproving nod.

Emma raised her eyebrows. 'Did he tell you that?' she asked.

The woman shifted uncomfortably. 'Well, not in so many words, but I overheard them talking about it. Our conservatories are very close together.'

Emma smiled inwardly. She could imagine Mrs Hurley lurking and listening to private conversations.

'They had many a discussion about it and I'm sure that's what eventually broke them up,' Mrs Hurley said, sipping her tea again. She gave a pointed look at Emma's cup on the side table and Emma pretended to take a hurried sip.

'I think you said she left him,' she said, putting down her cup as soon as she could.

Mrs Hurley pursed her lips again and nodded. 'There was

quite a to-do. I don't really know who decided to end the relationship but she took him to the cleaners and he was lucky to keep the house.'

'When did this happen?' Emma asked, writing down 'wife'.

Mrs Hurley paused. 'It was about seven years ago,' she said.

'Do you know her name or where she went?' This could be another avenue of investigation.

Mrs Hurley ignored her first question. Whether she didn't know or couldn't remember, Emma couldn't say. 'I never liked her so there was no reason to keep in touch. I felt so sorry for Martin. He was bereft for a long time after she went. Very independent though,' she added. 'I invited him to dinner lots of times, to save him from having to cook, but he insisted on carrying on alone.' Emma sensed how keen Martin Kendall would have been to stay away from Mrs Hurley's interrogations.

'Was his brother around a lot then?' she asked, sipping her tea. 'It sounds like the kind of time when family rally round.'

Mrs Hurley huffed. 'Him? He was never here then. I don't think they ever spoke during that time.'

'Did Martin tell you that?'

'He didn't have to. I saw for myself that his brother never darkened the door, even in Martin's hour of need.' She took a delicate sip from her cup. Emma admired her poise.

'When did Adrian start coming to visit?' she asked.

'A few years ago now. I think he moved back to Allensbury and they patched things up. Like I told you before, their relationship wasn't always amicable.' She frowned. 'At least not recently.'

Emma finished scribbling and looked up at her. 'You said you heard them arguing.'

'Yes. They were talking about money. Martin said he would help him out, so Adrian could do what he needed to do, but he didn't think it was a good idea.'

Emma frowned. 'The lending of money wasn't a good idea or Adrian doing what he wanted?'

Mrs Hurley shook her head. 'Doing what he wanted. From what I heard, it involved a woman.'

'Adrian had a woman?'

Mrs Hurley nodded. 'I assume so. He was saying he needed to help her, to get her away from there and Martin warned him that people had got hurt before.'

'What did you think had happened?' Emma asked, almost holding her breath.

Mrs Hurley shrugged. 'I assumed that Adrian was involved with a married woman and was trying to get her away from her husband.'

'Do you have any reason to think that Adrian was having an affair?' Emma asked.

Mrs Hurley waved a dismissive hand. 'You know what these acting types are like,' she said. 'You see it every day in the papers.' She wrinkled her nose. 'I'm sure it's his fault that Martin is dead.'

Emma raised her eyebrows. 'What makes you think that?'

Mrs Hurley leaned forward to put her cup and saucer on the table. 'Martin must have been doing something to help his brother; why else would he have been dressed as Santa? He would do anything to help a person in need and now he's paid the price for it.'

Chapter sixteen

'She thinks Martin was helping Adrian to cover up an affair?' Dan's voice was slightly muffled as it came through on Emma's car speakerphone, telling her that he was outside.

Emma nodded, even though he couldn't see her. 'She has absolutely no evidence for that apart from an eavesdropped conversation. She does *not* like Adrian at all, even though I suspect they've never even been introduced,' she said, negotiating her car out of Martin Kendall's street and heading back towards town. 'It was certainly worth the drive out here.'

Dan was silent a moment, then said, 'You're thinking Martin could have been killed by a jealous husband?'

'Yes, if we assume the husband knew that Adrian was Santa and didn't know what Adrian looked like.'

'What I don't get,' Dan said, 'is why wait until the night of the opening? There must have been other easier opportunities to kill him. Why then, when he was somewhere so public?'

Emma slowed for a roundabout then pulled out, taking the second exit for the town centre.

'He might have just found out what was going on. Maybe

it was the first chance he had while Adrian was alone. Who knows?'

'What are you going to do next?' Dan asked.

Emma frowned. 'I don't know. I've still not heard anything that confirms who the real target was.' She paused. 'What if,' she said slowly, 'they didn't just look alike, they sound alike as well?'

'Like you and your sister?' Dan asked.

'Exactly. Maybe Mrs Hurley overheard *Martin* saying he needed to help the woman escape?'

Dan sniffed. 'Would you not expect her to recognise her neighbour's voice?'

'Not if she couldn't see him. Shouldn't you be able to tell me and my sister apart on the phone?'

Dan laughed. 'True. Good job I didn't say anything saucy,' he said.

Emma grinned and braked for a red traffic light. 'I'm trying to consider all angles.'

'Clutching at straws?' Dan asked.

Emma glared at the phone attached to her dashboard as if it was Dan.

'Are you glaring at me?' he asked, laughing. When Emma didn't speak, he asked, 'Are you still there?'

She sighed. 'Yes, I'm thinking.'

'What are you going to do?'

Emma pulled away from the traffic lights and turned left. 'I'm going to talk to Martin's workmates and find out if he was seeing someone. If he wasn't, and there's no other reason why anyone would want to hurt him, then we go back to the theory that the killer was definitely after Adrian.'

***

It was clear the receptionist at Gateby and Sons was as nosy as Mrs Hurley when Emma asked if she could speak to someone about Martin Kendall. Her face wore a concerned expression but Emma could tell she was desperate to find out why an *Allensbury Post* reporter was asking about her dead colleague. Fortunately one of the firm's partners, Oliver Gateby, arrived just at that moment, smartly suited with a black leather briefcase clutched in his hand. Otherwise Emma suspected the woman would start shining a light in her eyes, demanding information.

'The young lady is asking about poor Martin,' the woman said, sounding more inquisitive than sympathetic. 'She's from the *Allensbury Post*.'

He turned to Emma. 'I see. Why are you asking about Martin?' he asked, his expression guarded.

'I'm doing a tribute piece and I'm speaking to friends and family about him,' she said, giving him her most engaging smile.

The man nodded. His bottom lip wobbled slightly and he cleared his throat. 'Come through,' he said in a slightly hoarse voice, gesturing towards a glass-fronted door. Emma followed him as he swiped a security card and pushed open the door. 'It's so sad about Martin,' he said, crossing the waiting room area and heading into a side office. It had a large window looking out onto the open plan section of the office floor where six people sat busily typing at computer keyboards.

Oliver pointed towards a round wooden table and four padded wooden chairs in the corner of the room. 'Have a seat.' He put down his briefcase and hung his overcoat and scarf on the coat stand by the door. Then he joined her at the table taking the chair opposite.

'What do you want to know about Martin?' he asked, leaning forward on the table surface and clasping his hands.

Emma pulled out her notebook and opened it to a blank page. 'What sort of man was he?' she asked.

'He was a good man,' Oliver said and then grimaced. 'God, that sounds clichéd, doesn't it? And it doesn't do him justice either.'

'In what way?'

Oliver frowned. 'It's hard to describe him really. He's been a friend for a long time, as long as we've both worked here and that's more years than I care to remember,' he said, pointing to the thinning grey curls on his head.

Emma smiled. 'I've spoken to a neighbour of his as well and she said he was very kind.'

Oliver smiled. 'I bet I can guess which neighbour,' he said. 'That woman was the bane of Martin's life, always sniffing around, poking her nose in where it wasn't wanted. He was still nice to her. I suppose that best characterises him. Patient and kind.'

Emma scribbled notes as he talked. 'How did you feel when you heard he'd been killed?' she asked, looking Oliver straight in the eyes.

His gaze dropped to the table and his bottom lip wobbled again. 'Devastated,' he said, his voice choked. He got to his feet and walked across to close the Venetian blinds over the glass front of his office before returning to his seat. 'Like I said, he was a good friend.'

Emma studied him carefully. 'Did you know his brother, Adrian?' she asked.

Tears glistened in Oliver's eyes. 'No, not really. I've met him a few times since he moved back to Allensbury. He'd been living in London. He's an actor. He and Martin didn't speak much, until he came back to Allensbury.'

'Was Martin pleased he'd come back?'

Oliver nodded, smiling again. 'He was. They reconciled pretty quickly when Adrian moved here, so I think Martin had been hoping for it all these years. It was a bit like the prodigal son.'

Emma smiled. 'The best reception Adrian could have had,' she said.

Oliver looked down at his clasped hands. 'He caused Martin a lot of stress though,' he said. 'Martin never said what it was but I know it wasn't all plain sailing.'

'Adrian needed money?' Emma asked.

Oliver frowned. 'No, well, at least not at first. He'd managed to save while he was working and he was living in a very cheap area of town. Such as there is one in Allensbury.'

Emma nodded. 'The neighbour said they argued a lot. She seemed to think it was because Adrian needed money.'

'I didn't think it was money he wanted, more Martin's help and advice. There was something going on although Martin wouldn't tell me what it was.'

'Mrs Hurley – Martin's neighbour – seemed to think that Adrian had a woman and that might have been causing trouble.'

Oliver smiled. 'That wouldn't surprise me,' he said. 'Adrian was an attractive man. I could easily see him getting into a scrape over a woman.'

'What about Martin?' Emma asked. 'Was he seeing anyone?'

'Why would you ask that?' Oliver asked, suddenly guarded.

'He was a good looking man.' Emma smiled and Oliver smiled back.

'Adrian and Martin looked very alike,' she continued. Oliver nodded. 'Did they sound alike?'

Oliver considered a moment. 'Possibly, a little.'

'Given that Martin was killed, I wondered whether Mrs Hurley had heard *him* talking about a woman rather than Adrian.'

There was a slight pause. 'I don't think so,' Oliver said. 'I would know if there was a woman on the scene.'

Worried that she was going too far, Emma decided to change tack. 'Did you know Martin's wife?' she said.

Oliver nodded. 'Yes. Not a very nice woman, as it happens.'

'Mrs Hurley seemed to think they split up because Martin wanted children and his wife didn't.'

Oliver sighed and put his face in his hands. 'That bloody woman,' he said, his voice muffled. 'Always snooping.'

'It wasn't because they disagreed over children?' Emma asked.

'No.' Oliver looked up, the tears back in his eyes. 'They split up because Martin had started seeing someone else.'

'Who?' Emma asked, pen poised, waiting for a new avenue of investigation to open up.

'Me,' said Oliver, as the tears started down his cheeks.

Chapter seventeen

At five o'clock Emma was loitering in the alley that joined Fenleys to the multi-storey car park. She was waiting by the staff exit for Lotte Clarke. A quick call to Lydia had confirmed this was when Lotte finished her shift.

'Why do you want to know that?' Lydia had asked, voice dripping with curiosity, before releasing the information.

'I need to speak to her, that's all,' Emma had replied.

'She's on the shop floor. Why not talk to her now?'

'This has to be done in private,' Emma said. She immediately regretted the words, knowing Lydia wouldn't let that go.

'I'll only tell you if you agree to tell me what you find out later,' Lydia had said, and Emma could tell she was going to have to accept Lydia's request.

'Is that not blackmail?' she'd asked, impressed by Lydia's doggedness.

'Of course, but no one else will believe I'd do that,' Lydia had replied.

Emma had to laugh. She'd never thought she'd have that kind of talk with Lydia.

She was still turning her conversation with Oliver Gateby over in her mind as she stood in the freezing cold wind that whistled down the alley, hoping that Lotte was the sort of person to leave dead on time. Just as she felt that her feet would fall off, despite being encased in winter boots and thick socks, Lotte emerged from the door, zipping up her winter coat. She started back in alarm when Emma stepped forward to greet her.

'What do you want?' she demanded, crossing her arms and adopting an aggressive stance.

'I want to talk to you about Adrian Kendall.'

Lotte's eyes widened. 'I don't know Adrian Kendall,' she said, turning away towards the car park.

'Wait.' Emma put a hand on Lotte's arm but the latter winced and shook it off. 'I know you're friends. I saw you coming out of his flat yesterday. You have a key.'

Lotte turned back so suddenly that Emma took a couple of steps backwards. 'How do you know that? Are you following me?'

Emma held up her palms in surrender. 'I was looking for Adrian so I went to his flat. I'm trying to find out what happened to his brother.'

Lotte's arms folded again. 'Why do you want Adrian? He had nothing to do with his brother's murder.'

'Lotte, it was supposed to be Adrian in the Santa suit. He might have been the real target, and if I can find out for sure he can come out of hiding.'

Lotte's hands dropped to her sides and were then shoved into her coat pockets. 'He doesn't know anything about Martin's murder,' she insisted. 'He doesn't know whether he was the real target so he can't tell you anything.'

'Where is he? I need to talk to him.'

Lotte shook her head. 'He won't talk to anyone.'

'What about the police? They're appealing for him to come forward. Will he talk to them?'

Lotte said nothing.

'Look,' Emma said, 'even if he wasn't the real target, does he not want to know who killed his brother? The sooner he talks, the sooner we can work it out and he'll be safe.'

'He's safe enough where he is.' Lotte's lips were in a firm line. 'He doesn't need your help.'

Emma opened her mouth to speak, but Lotte had glanced up the street and she went very still.

'You have to go,' she said. 'Go now.' She grabbed Emma's elbow and gave her a push towards the car park. 'Go.'

Emma looked over her shoulder and saw Helena barrelling down the alley towards them. She quickened her pace and heard Helena demand 'who was that?' and heard a sharp intake of breath from Lotte. Another glance over her shoulder showed Helena with Lotte's arm in a vice-like grip. She heard Lotte insisting that Emma was a shopper who had stopped to ask the time, that she didn't know her.

Not wanting to cause more trouble, Emma hurried across the ground floor of the multi-storey car park, through the side door and into the street.

Chapter eighteen

When Emma joined Lydia in a cosy corner of The Tavern, the latter was halfway down a large glass of Pinot Grigio. A bottle rested in an ice bucket on the table alongside a second empty glass and two packets of crisps. Emma took off her coat, folded it and laid it on the banquette before sitting down. She nodded to the bottle.

'You started without me,' she said, with a grin.

Lydia snorted. 'It's been that sort of day.' She picked up the bottle and sloshed some wine into the other glass. She pushed it across the table to Emma who picked it up, raised it in a silent toast and took a sip.

'So,' Lydia said, leaning forward on the table, 'why did I help you to ambush Lotte as she left work today?'

Emma thought for a moment and then told Lydia about seeing Lotte outside Adrian's flat having locked up with a key.

Lydia gaped. 'What? She had a key?'

Emma nodded. 'The reason I wanted to speak to her was to find out why, and where Adrian is now.'

Lydia sat back and puffed out a breath, making her fringe

flutter. 'Well, that explains what I saw the other day,' she said. Emma raised her eyebrows. 'I saw them coming out of the Italian café down the road. They looked quite cosy and hugged before they went their separate ways.'

'You think they're in a relationship?' Emma asked.

Lydia wrinkled her nose. 'I don't know. They didn't kiss or anything, which you'd expect if they were a couple.'

Emma frowned and fiddled with her wine glass. 'I think Lotte knows where Adrian is, although she's not giving anything away. I tried saying that he could be a target, that I'm trying to find out who killed Martin, but she wouldn't budge. Says Adrian is safe and doesn't know anything.'

Lydia sighed heavily. 'It's a no-go there then,' she said, and Emma nodded.

'I'll find a way though.' She paused. 'How did it go with the police this morning?'

'It was horrible. They just kept going over and over the same thing: I'd been cross with Adrian; he was almost late; how did I feel about that, etcetera etcetera.' She took a very un-Lydia-like gulp of wine. 'Then they asked me about a secret, who I'd been talking to backstage about a secret.' She swirled the wine gently in her glass. 'I don't know how they found out about that.'

Emma played with her glass's stem. 'Tony Cootes overheard you.'

Lydia looked shocked. 'How do you know that?'

Emma took a sip. 'He told me.'

'I can't believe he'd tell the police before mentioning it to me. I thought he liked me.' Lydia's bottom lip wobbled.

Emma frowned. 'I suspect he's trying to cover his own back. He told me that he went back into the store to get his phone, just before the opening. If he heard your conversation, then he was close enough to the backstage area,' Emma said, resting her elbows on the table and leaning forward.

'I didn't see him backstage,' Lydia said, shaking her head. 'I'd stepped into the staff-only corridor nearby; I didn't shut the door.'

'Without you actually in the backstage area, he could have snuck in, couldn't he?'

Lydia frowned. 'Why would Tony want to kill Martin?'

'Martin in the Santa suit looked like Adrian, remember,' Emma pointed out, taking a few crisps. 'It would be easy to confuse them.' She shoved the crisps in her mouth and wiped her hands on her trousers. 'Who do you think this is?' She picked up her phone, found a photograph and held it up to Lydia.

Lydia peered at the screen. 'That's Adrian,' she said.

'Nope, that's Martin,' Emma said, slightly smugly. Lydia stared at her. 'They could be twins, couldn't they?' Emma said.

Lydia took a deep breath and puffed out her cheeks. 'That certainly puts a different slant on it, doesn't it?' she asked.

Emma nodded. 'The question is, when you found the body and Tony rushed in to help you, where had he come from?' she said, picking up two more crisps.

'I assumed he was outside,' Lydia said, 'but he did arrive very quickly.'

'So he could have been inside the shop?' Emma asked.

Lydia nodded. 'He rushed in, pulled me away and started checking for a pulse. Then when other people came in he told them all to get back. Maybe he was just trying to preserve the crime scene.' Her shoulders drooped when she saw the dubious expression on Emma's face. 'You think he killed Martin thinking it was Adrian? Then how did Martin get into the window?'

Emma frowned. 'He probably staggered away once he'd been

stabbed, trying to escape, and went into the window.' She stopped, feeling a tightening in her chest. 'He mustn't have had anywhere else to go,' she said quietly.

She and Lydia looked at each other silently for a moment.

Then Emma took a big drink of wine. 'You say you didn't have anything to do with killing Martin but I know you're hiding something,' she said, looking at Lydia, whose eyes suddenly became fixed on the table. 'What is it, Lydia? What were you doing?'

Lydia sighed heavily. 'I was on the phone—' she began.

Emma frowned at her. 'That's your big secret? For God's sake, there's no reason to hide that. Whoever you were talking to can vouch for you. They could—'

'No, I can't ask him to do that,' Lydia interrupted.

'Are you mad?' Emma gasped. 'You could be facing a murder charge. I'm sure they would help.'

Lydia took a gulp of wine and set down her glass. 'His name is Will,' she said quietly.

Emma, in the act of taking a sip herself, spluttered into her wine glass. 'Will?' she demanded. 'Who's Will?' When Lydia said nothing, Emma continued, 'Are you cheating on Ed?'

'No,' Lydia cried. Then she said, 'Well, not really.'

Emma wiped her chin with the back of her hand. 'Not really? What does *that* mean?'

'I met Will through that yoga course I've been doing. We went for a drink one night after the lesson and got talking.'

Emma raised her eyebrows. 'Does Ed know about him?'

Lydia's mouth turned down at the corners and she shook her head.

'Are you actually going out with him?' Emma asked, taking a crisp from the packet and nibbling it.

Lydia fiddled with the stem of her glass. 'We've been sort of seeing each other for the last month. We've kissed a few times as well. He keeps calling and texting.' She looked up and saw Emma's shocked expression.

'He called you right before the opening, just as you were waiting for Adrian to arrive?' Emma asked.

'Yes. Then I saw what I thought was Adrian and I had to get him off the phone. I told him we'd speak later and I ended the call.'

'You need to end more than just the call, if you ask me,' Emma said, taking a big swig.

'You won't tell Ed, will you?' Lydia asked, sounding panicked. 'Or Dan? He'd tell Ed for sure.'

Emma shook her head but there was a knot in the pit of her stomach. 'It's none of my business.' She stopped and puffed out her cheeks. 'You definitely didn't see anyone else backstage or in the shop?'

Lydia shook her head. 'There were a few shoppers around, but most people had gone outside for the opening. I was only a few feet away. In all honesty, I wasn't really concentrating on looking out for people. I was trying to get Will off the phone. The only person I really saw was what I thought was Adrian passing.'

Emma sat back in her seat and took another gulp. She overdid it and spilt some on her chin and down the front of her shirt. She wiped her hand across her face to dry it and dug in her handbag for a tissue, blushing. When she looked up, Lydia was watching her.

'When you've finished taking a wine bath,' she said, her lips pulling up slightly as she fought not to laugh. 'What do you think is going on?'

'I don't know. However, I think another conversation with

Tony Cootes is in order, to find out exactly where he was when Martin was killed.'

Chapter nineteen

A late council meeting for Dan meant that Emma wasn't able to give him an update until Thursday morning. He stared at Emma opened mouthed as she recounted her conversation with Oliver Gateby. They were standing in the car park behind the *Post*'s building away from prying ears.

'I didn't see that one coming,' he said when she'd finished.

Emma nodded. 'I doubt his neighbour would be quite so friendly if she knew the truth,' she said. 'She seems like that sort of person.'

Dan sighed. 'That blows your theory about the angry husband,' he said.

'Not necessarily. We now know that it wasn't an angry husband after *Martin*, so we're back to the idea that he was looking for Adrian and got the wrong man.'

'Are you going to tell anyone about Oliver and Martin?' Dan asked.

Emma shook her head. 'It's their private business. I told Oliver I'll only quote him as Martin's colleague.' She looked down at the ground. 'I felt so sorry for him and for making him cry. I left him my whole packet of tissues.'

'It's not your fault,' Dan said.

Emma took a deep breath and looked up at Dan. 'Well, it's made me more determined to find the killer. Oliver deserves to know why his partner died, especially because it seems like it wasn't Martin's fault.'

'Are you going to look for Martin's wife?' Dan asked.

Emma shook her head. 'They split up years ago and it sounds like she got her pound of flesh at the time. Why would she have come back again now?'

'Is there any chance you can use your considerable powers of persuasion to make Lotte tell you where Adrian is hiding?' Dan asked.

Emma groaned. 'No, she was a closed book. I think it will take a miracle to get those pages open now.'

She turned and led the way into the building. As she arrived at her desk, the phone began to ring. She grabbed the receiver.

'Hi, Suzy,' she said when the police press officer identified herself.

'I need your help,' came the uncharacteristically brusque reply.

Emma straightened up and picked up her pen. 'Go ahead.'

'We're struggling to get hold of Adrian Kendall,' Suzy said. 'Can you do an appeal for him to come forward?'

Emma nodded. 'Of course,' she said, writing Suzy's name and date at the top of her notebook page. 'He's still not at home?' she asked.

There was a sigh. 'Which you know because you've already been there,' Suzy said, sounding resigned.

Emma smiled to herself. 'It was for the usual tribute piece. You didn't tell me I couldn't speak to him.' She frowned. 'And he's still not come forward? Not even to identify his brother's body?' Emma asked, pen poised.

'No, one of Martin's work colleagues came to do that. We'd initially contacted Adrian's boss at Fenleys but he said he didn't know Martin. He was really shocked by the news though.'

Emma paused. She still couldn't be sure whether Tony Cootes's shock was genuine or more like guilt that he'd killed the wrong man.

'If the ID has been done, why do you still need Adrian? Do you think he was involved in his brother's death?' Emma asked, holding her breath. There was a silence on the other end of the line. 'Suzy? Are you still there?'

'We just need to speak to him,' Suzy said, her voice guarded.

'Do you think he had something to do with Martin's death?' Emma asked, an idea striking her. Would Adrian have hurt his brother when the neighbour and Oliver Gateby seemed to think they were close?

There was a silence at the other end of the line. 'We just need to get him to come forward.'

'Have you spoken to Lotte Clarke? She works at Fenleys,' Emma said.

'The woman who found the murder weapon?' Suzy asked slowly.

'Yes, it seems she's mates with Adrian so she might be able to help you.'

Suzy gave a sharp intake of breath. 'How do you know that? No one else has mentioned it.'

'When I went to his flat I saw her coming out with a holdall and locking the door with a key.'

'She had a key?'

'Yes. When I asked her about it she got all awkward and

wouldn't tell me where he is. She said he was safe and won't talk to anyone.' She could hear Suzy typing a note to herself.

'When did you find this out?' Suzy asked.

Emma doodled some triangles on her notebook. 'Yesterday. Well, I went to the flat on Tuesday, but only managed to catch up with her yesterday when she was finishing work.'

'Thanks. That's really helpful.' She heard a loud tap as if Suzy had finished the sentence she was typing.

'Is there anything else you can tell me about Martin's death?' Emma asked, joining two triangles with a straight line.

'Off the record?'

Emma put down her pen. 'Of course.'

Suzy took a deep breath. 'We found blood in the backstage area, so it's likely that Martin was already in costume when he was stabbed. We think he went into the window to try to escape his killer.'

A cold feeling seemed to have lodged in Emma's chest as she imagined Martin Kendall's last moments.

'It was probably the only way he could go,' she whispered.

'That's the theory we're working on,' Suzy said, sounding as if she was feeling the same as Emma. Both were silent.

'Were there any witnesses?' Emma asked, regaining the use of her voice.

'None that we've found so far. It seems like everyone was out the front for the window opening.'

'The shop can't have been entirely empty,' Emma said. 'Someone must have seen something. What about CCTV from inside the store?'

'Not that we've found so far. There's a lot to go through. It looks like the killer may have known where the cameras were. If you can make an appeal for witnesses, including his brother, that would be great,' Suzy said.

'No problem. Do you have any theories about why Martin was targeted?' Emma asked.

'We're still investigating so I can't comment on that yet.' Suzy slipped back into her official statement voice. 'I need you to report that we're looking for anyone who was in or around the shop in the thirty minutes before the window opening to come forward. If you can lead with the call for Adrian to come forward that would be great. I'll pass the info about Lotte Clarke on to the team on the case. They might want to speak to you about it directly.'

'No problem. Just ask them to call me. Is there anything else?'

'I've got nothing else, but I'll keep you posted. I'll get those quotes to you in the next thirty minutes hopefully. Can you let me know when the piece is going out so we can be ready for calls?'

'Certainly.' Emma said goodbye, put down the phone and took a deep breath. Apart from Lotte Clarke, it seemed no one had heard from or seen Adrian Kendall since before his brother was killed. From what she'd heard of Adrian it didn't sound likely that he would kill his brother, but maybe – when he arrived late for the opening – he'd seen who did. She needed to find him quickly, before the police had him in custody. She had questions only he could answer.

Chapter twenty

Feeling that she'd had a long few days Emma decided to treat herself to a cappuccino and a Panini from the cosy delicatessen on the corner of the street. As she waited for her order to be completed, her mobile burst into life, playing a jaunty rendition of her favourite nineties tune. She looked at the screen and saw that it was forwarded from her desk phone.

'Hello?'

'You're looking for me,' a man's voice said.

Emma frowned. 'Sorry? Who is this?' she asked.

'Adrian Kendall.'

The phone almost slipped out of her hand. 'Mr Kendall, you're a hard man to find.' She sat down at an empty table and scrabbled in her bag for her notebook. 'Did Lotte tell you that I'd like to—'

'I can't talk here,' he interrupted. 'I'll tell you everything but not here. Not on the phone.'

'Where are you?'

'I said I can't talk here. We need to meet.'

'Sure. Where?'

There was a pause on the other end of the line.

'Mr Kendall? Are you still there?' Emma asked, fearing that he'd hung up.

'Castle Park in Allensbury, by the boating lake in an hour. There's a shed where they store the boats. Come alone and don't tell anyone you've spoken to me.'

'If you know something about your brother's death, then—'

'Not here,' Adrian Kendall snapped. 'I'll tell you everything when I see you.'

And the phone went dead.

So much for a nice quiet lunch. Emma returned to the counter and asked for her coffee and Panini to be wrapped up to take away. Her head was rattling with all the questions she wanted to ask. Primarily, who would want to kill him and why they had not succeeded?

***

Before she could go and meet Adrian Kendall, Emma had to go back to the office. She had copy to file if she was going to keep Daisy sweet. She was glad she'd made that decision when the snow began to fall heavily, but she was now trying to type so fast that she kept making mistakes. Trying to eat the Panini and drink her coffee was adding a complication to the process. After she swore for the third time under her breath, the news editor came across to her desk.

'What are you muttering about?' Daisy asked, sitting down in Dan's vacant chair. 'There's no need to type so fast.'

'There is,' Emma replied without stopping. 'I've got something big.'

Daisy frowned. 'What do you mean?' she asked, leaning an elbow on Dan's desk.

Emma finished typing, scanned the words for typos and pressed 'send' to forward her story to the news desk email box. She took a deep breath.

'Adrian Kendall rang me. He wants to tell me everything. He's scared.'

Daisy stared at her. 'And he wants to talk to you rather than the police? Why?'

'I don't know. He wants to meet me in the park to talk,' Emma said, 'in about fifteen minutes, so I gotta go.' She clicked a few keys to lock her computer and switched off her monitor. Throwing her notebook and two pens into her handbag, she stood up.

'You're not going on your own,' Daisy said. 'I'll send one of the juniors with you.'

Emma shook her head. 'If he sees anyone else he's going to bolt. I've got to go alone.'

Daisy stood up and folded her arms. 'Right, exactly where are you going?' Emma told her and received a nod in response. 'You call me in twenty minutes or I send out a search party, all right?'

Emma nodded. 'If I've not got him to talk by then, I'll take him to the police myself.'

***

When Emma got outside and felt the temperature, she was glad she'd decided to wait out the hour in the office. There were still flurries of snow in the air and a couple of slushy centimetres underfoot. She'd have frozen to death by now if she'd waited outside. Pulling on her woolly hat and her gloves, she walked down the steps outside the building.

She quickly wound through the streets towards the park, passing under the balcony of Dan and Ed's flat. Was it foolish to go without back up? She was about to pull out her phone and call or text Dan when she shook herself. Adrian wasn't going to hurt her. He needed her.

She passed through the park gates. The rules said it closed at dusk and a quick glance at the sky showed her that it probably wouldn't be long before that happened. The leaden grey sky suggested they were soon in for another blizzard.

Emma crossed the grass to the boating lake, her feet slipping and sliding on the snowy ground. Several hardy people with dogs were out for a walk and several ducks waddled about on the frozen lake surface quacking constantly to each other, as if complaining about the weather. Emma shivered and huddled into her coat. She couldn't see anyone standing near the shed. Swinging her arms to keep warm, she turned on the spot. As she looked at a copse of trees off to her right, she thought she could see a dark shape. Adrian might be sheltering in there. She began to walk towards it.

A figure emerged, one hand clutching at a tree branch and the other pressed to his chest. Emma's steps faltered. Then she began to run as the figure dropped to the ground. She reached the man and found herself looking at Adrian Kendall, a dark-red stain spreading across the pale-blue roll neck jumper he was wearing under an open Barbour quilted jacket. She dropped to her knees, dragging off her scarf and pressing it against the wound. Her other hand scrabbled in her bag for her mobile phone. Gripping the fingers in her teeth, she dragged off a glove and dialled 999.

'Hang on, Adrian, just hang on,' she said, hoping she sounded reassuring. His lips moved and she leaned down towards him but his voice was too soft to hear. 'Ambulance please,' she said when the phone was answered. Adrian was still trying to speak. 'Adrian, I can't hear you,' she said, ears straining. When the voice on the phone asked for her location, Emma started to explain but she'd barely got the words out when she felt a heavy thump on her head and white lights popped before her eyes. She slumped to the ground and the last thing she saw before she passed out was a pair of leather boots.

Chapter twenty-one

The next thing Emma knew she was lying face down, her cheek resting in the shallow snow. She lifted her head and looked around. There was no one there. So who had hit her? She rested her forehead on the snowy ground again for a moment, trying to clear her foggy brain.

Glancing to her left she saw Adrian Kendall lying on the snowy grass, not moving. She struggled onto her hands and knees, crawled to him, and shook his shoulder.

'Adrian?' she croaked. 'Mr Kendall, wake up.'

Then she heard a voice yell her name. She looked up and saw Dan and Ed sprinting across the snowy grass towards her. She continued to shake Adrian and call his name as they arrived, panting. Dan dropped to his knees, trying to move her away from the sprawled figure.

'Em, what the hell is going on?' he demanded, wrapping his arms around her as Emma struggled to return to Adrian. Ed was pulling out his phone.

'I think I've already called an ambulance,' she said, sounding slightly slurred.

'I'll call and check,' Ed responded, dialling, as Dan dragged off his coat and wrapped it carefully around Emma, giving her a kiss on the cheek. An *Allensbury Post* beanie replaced her soaked woolly hat and Dan's scarf was wound around her neck. Dan couldn't find his gloves, so Ed's were donated to the cause.

She gestured towards Adrian. 'Help him. He's bleeding really badly.'

Dan crawled across the snowy ground to Adrian and began to shake him. 'Adrian? Adrian, can you hear me?' he asked.

Emma sank back onto the ground. 'Where did you two come from?'

'We're Daisy's search party,' Dan said, trying to poke his fingers inside Adrian's collar to check for a pulse.

Emma huddled into the coat as Ed returned, pocketing his phone. 'There's a first responder already on his way,' he said, 'and he shouldn't be long.'

'I think it might be too late,' Dan said, fingers still feeling around Adrian's neck. 'He's so cold, I can't tell if there's a pulse.'

Ed dragged off his coat and scarf, showing off a thick woolly jumper underneath. 'Cover him with those. I'm going to wait at the park gates for the paramedic.' Dan nodded and Ed marched away across the grass.

'Is he OK?' Emma demanded, pointing to Adrian.

Dan looked up at her. 'I don't know. He seems to have lost a lot of blood.' He gestured to the growing red stain on Adrian's jumper.

Emma could feel tears starting in her eyes. 'You need to help him.'

Dan tried to tuck Ed's coat around Adrian. 'I don't think lying in the snow is doing him, or you, any good,' he said. 'Can you move into there?' He pointed to the copse of trees. 'That might shelter you from the cold a bit.'

Emma shook her head. 'I'm not sure I can get up,' she said, tears running down her face. She raised a hand to wipe them away and found that her gloved hands were already wet and shaking.

Dan crawled to her and wrapped his arms around her. 'I thought you were dead,' he said, voice shaking. 'I saw you lying on the ground and I was so scared. I thought you were both dead.'

Emma pressed her face into his chest, beginning to sob.

'What happened?' Dan asked, squeezing her.

'I was waiting by the shed when Adrian came staggering out of the trees, bleeding,' Emma gasped, 'and when I went to help him, someone hit me over the head.'

She felt her teeth start chattering and she was shaking uncontrollably.

'We need to get you indoors,' Dan said, trying to share his body heat with her and failing. Snow was falling heavier and they were both soaked. He was starting to shiver without a coat. He looked up and said, 'Ah, here's Ed.'

Ed approached with two uniformed police officers and the paramedic, weighed down with a load of kit.

The paramedic knelt beside Adrian, unwrapping him to make his examination and handing Ed his coat. The latter didn't put it on, examining it carefully for blood stains.

'Is he dead?' Emma asked in a shaky voice.

The paramedic looked up and nodded. 'There's nothing you could have done, love,' he said, pointing to Adrian's jumper as tears continued to run down Emma's face. 'It looks like a deep wound and he's lost a lot of blood.'

'Let's head back to the flat. We need to get you warmed up,'

Dan said, standing up and pulling Emma gently to her feet. She swayed against him.

The paramedic got to his feet too. 'I need to check her over,' he said, gesturing to Emma.

'It's not far,' Dan said, pointing to their block of flats. The paramedic nodded and picked up his bags. Ed took one and the man smiled gratefully.

'Don't worry,' said one of the police officers as the other spoke quickly into his radio. 'We'll wait for back-up here and pop along to take a statement when we can.'

Dan gave them the address and the officer scribbled it in his notebook.

With Dan's arm wrapped tightly around her, Emma set off across the grass feeling as if she was floating, followed by Ed and the paramedic.

***

Dan and Ed watched as the paramedic undid the blood pressure cuff from around Emma's arm. This was difficult as she was still trembling. But the hoody and tracksuit bottoms she'd borrowed from Dan while her own clothes were hung up to dry were starting to work their magic. The kettle could be heard boiling in the kitchen. There was a click and Ed left the room.

Dan sat down on the armchair opposite Emma. 'What's the verdict?' he asked the paramedic as the man flashed a penlight in Emma's eyes.

'Clean bill of health,' the paramedic said, smiling up at Emma. 'No sign of concussion at the moment, but you need to rest up. Plenty of warm drinks and if there's any dizziness or feeling sick, you take her to the hospital,' he said, looking up at Dan. He got to his feet and had started to pack up when Ed came in and put three mugs of tea on the table.

'Do you want one?' he asked the paramedic.

The man reached a hand into his bag and pulled out a flask. 'I don't suppose you could...' he asked, holding it out to Ed.

Ed grinned. 'No problem,' he said, taking the flask and returning to the kitchen with one of the mugs. They heard splashing as the tea was poured into the flask. Ed returned and handed it back.

'Thanks.' The man smiled, stowing the flask back in his bag.

Once he'd finished putting away his kit, Dan thanked him, showed him out, and returned to the living room. He stood in the doorway with his arms folded, looking from Emma to Ed and back again.

'Whoever wanted to kill Adrian has succeeded now,' he stated.

Emma's eyes filled with tears and she pressed her hands to her face. Dan crossed the room and sat beside her, putting an arm around her. She leaned into him and began to sob. He held her close and whispered comforting words in her ear that she didn't really hear. Eventually she took a deep breath and tried to pull herself together. 'He tried to tell me something,' she whimpered. 'I couldn't hear what it was. Then someone hit me over the head.'

'Did you see them?' Ed asked, sitting down on the armchair.

Emma shook her head and sniffed. 'All I saw was a pair of leather boots. I can't remember anything else.'

'Men's or women's?' Dan asked.

'I couldn't tell you,' Emma said, digging in her cardigan sleeve for a tissue. She wiped her eyes and blew her nose.

Ed got up and disappeared into the kitchen, returning with a kitchen roll. He handed it to Emma who pulled off a sheet and blew her nose again.

'Thanks,' she said. 'It all happened so quickly I didn't see anything apart from a pair of boots.' She leaned forward and picked up her tea mug, gripping it with both hands. She had almost stopped shivering and the tea stayed in the mug. 'I can't believe he's dead and I couldn't do anything to help.' Tears threatened again and she wiped them away with a hand.

'You heard the paramedic,' Dan said, stroking her back, 'he'd lost a lot of blood before you found him. There was nothing you could have done.'

'But now we're back to the question of who would want to kill Adrian Kendall?' Ed said, looking from Dan to Emma.

She nodded. 'Martin was in Adrian's costume when he was killed, and then when the killer realised he'd killed the wrong man, he hunted Adrian down and made sure this time.'

'Why did Adrian try to tell you whatever it was and not the police?' Ed asked. 'They would have protected him.'

Emma shook her head, feeling tears start in her eyes. 'I don't know.' She sniffed. 'Why didn't I tell him to go straight to the police station instead?' she asked, looking at Dan and Ed. 'If I'd done that he would still be alive.' Tears began to roll down her face again.

'Hey, come on,' Dan said gently, taking the mug from her hands and putting it on the table, 'you can't think like that. He was an adult; it's on him to decide what he was doing.'

Emma pressed her face into his shoulder and cried, Dan squeezing her and rubbing her back.

'Adrian was a nice guy who plays Santa for the kids and does panto,' she sobbed. 'Why would someone want to kill him?'

Dan and Ed looked at each other over her head. Ed sat back in the armchair. When neither spoke, Emma looked up.

'You think he had a dark side?' she asked.

Dan continued to pat her back as she fought to control herself. She sat up straight and dried her face on her cardigan sleeve.

'We don't really know anything about him,' Ed said, leaning forward and handing her a piece of kitchen roll. 'Lydia said he was a private guy. He was always nice to people and chatted to them but never gave much away.'

'It sounds like he knew Lotte Clarke pretty well,' Dan said. 'She has a key to his flat.'

Emma picked up her tea mug and blew on the surface. 'Lydia said she saw them having a cosy coffee together and hugging,' she said. 'That certainly suggests some kind of relationship.'

'Hopefully the police will be gentle when they break the news,' Dan said, sitting back in the sofa and rubbing her back.

Emma looked at him puzzled and then twigged what he meant. 'I'm glad I told Suzy about her because at least then they'll know to go and speak to her and let her know he's gone.'

'Do you think she'll talk to you about Adrian now?' Ed asked.

Emma took a deep breath. 'I can try. She might know whether there's a reason why someone would want to kill Adrian.' She tried to stand up but fell back against the cushions.

Dan frowned at her. 'Not tonight you're not,' he said. 'You're staying here and resting.'

'Yes, Doctor Sullivan.' Emma pouted.

Dan laughed. 'We all need a hot dinner,' he said, looking up at Ed. The latter nodded.

'I'll get us a curry,' he said, pulling out his wallet and checking for cash. Then he fetched a takeaway menu. Emma watched distractedly as Dan and Ed debated the benefits of a bhuna versus a madras for warming Emma up quickly. If only she could remember more about those boots. She rubbed the back of her head, wincing when her fingers touched the lump that had swollen up.

Then the takeaway menu was thrust under her nose and she decided to come back to thinking later.

Chapter twenty-two

A detective arrived at Dan and Ed's flat on Friday morning to interview Emma.

She introduced herself as Sophie Madison and declined Dan's offer of a hot drink. Then she sat down opposite Emma. Dan excused himself and left the room.

'How are you?' Madison asked.

Emma shrugged. 'I don't know,' she said. 'I didn't get much sleep last night. I just kept seeing him lying there.' She wrapped her arms around herself, suddenly feeling cold.

Madison nodded. 'I'm not surprised,' she said, smiling encouragingly at Emma. 'Can you tell me exactly what happened?' she asked.

Emma told the woman about the call from Adrian, going to the park, and finding him bleeding.

'But you say you don't know him?' Madison asked.

Emma shook her head. 'I've never met him but I knew who he was. I'd been writing about his brother's murder.'

Madison nodded. 'Why did you go and meet him in the park?'

'He called me and asked to meet. He said he was going to tell me everything.'

'What did you understand by that?' Madison asked, scribbling in her notebook.

Emma shrugged. 'At first I thought he was going to tell me why someone would kill his brother or whether the knife was originally meant for him. Later I wondered whether he'd seen something when Martin was killed.'

Madison frowned. 'Why would you think that?' she asked.

Emma explained about Adrian's poor timekeeping. 'I just thought maybe he was late for the opening and he saw whoever killed Martin. That's why he was in hiding.' She clasped her hands on her lap. 'Do you know who did it?' she asked. 'Who killed Martin and Adrian?'

Madison shook her head. 'Not yet but we're making progress.' She looked down at her notebook, her face impassive. Then she looked back at Emma. 'You told Suzy in the press office that we should talk to Lotte Clarke. Why was that?'

Emma told Madison about seeing Lotte coming out of Adrian's flat after it was revealed that Adrian was still alive. 'When I asked her about it she got all defensive, said Adrian was safe and he wouldn't talk to anyone. I told her to get him to come forward even if it was just to find out who killed Martin.'

'Was she in a relationship with Adrian Kendall?' the detective asked, looking up at Emma, pen poised.

'I didn't initially think they had anything to do with each other. I've since heard from one person that she'd seen them hugging and going for a cosy coffee,' Emma said, pulling her sleeves down over her hands.

Madison said nothing, eyes focused on the notebook as she continued to scribble.

Then she looked up. 'Is there anything else you need to tell me?'

Emma thought for a moment and then shook her head.

Madison clicked away the nib of her pen and pushed it and her notebook into her coat pocket. From another pocket she pulled out a business card. 'If you think of anything else' – she held it out – 'just give me a call.'

Emma took the card, nodding, and got to her feet. 'I will, thanks,' she said.

As Madison walked out of the room, she looked back at Emma. 'You've done a good job of investigating so far, but you've also been injured. Please leave this to us now. We don't want you getting hurt again.'

Emma nodded, showed her out and returned to the living room.

Dan had reappeared. 'I heard that last bit,' he said. 'Are you giving up investigating?'

'Hell, no,' Emma replied, finding her handbag beside the sofa and checking that everything she needed was inside.

'That's my girl. What's your next step?'

Emma frowned. 'I need to speak to Lotte Clarke again before the police get to her.'

***

After finding out from Lydia that Lotte had called in sick, Emma made use of an online phone book to find Lotte and Helena's address in the north side of Allensbury. As she navigated her way onto their housing development, she realised that it wasn't very far away from Martin Kendall's house.

She turned her car at the end of the cul-de-sac and pulled up outside the house two doors down. The Clarkes' house was a lot smaller than Martin's place but no less well kept. The front garden of chipped slate was immaculate, with no weeds poking out. The potted shrubs were neatly clipped and there were no weeds growing between the slabs of the driveway either. There was no car parked at the front of the house although Emma could see the television playing in what she assumed was the front room. Someone was home.

She walked up the short path to the front door and rang the doorbell. After a minute or so, getting no answer, she pushed the bell again. There was no sound of anyone moving around. She stepped onto the slate garden and peered through the living room window. Leather sofas sat on a laminated wood floor; a wooden coffee table stood on a rug between the sofa and the large TV that hung on the wall. There were no magazines or books visible or ornaments on shelves. Very show-home, Emma thought. A large canvas bearing a photograph of Helena and Lotte hung on the wall. The former was beaming, her arms clasped around her daughter.

She stepped back to the front door and pushed open the letter box.

'Lotte?' she called. 'Lotte, are you in there? It's Emma. We met at Fenleys.' She waited half a minute and tried again. 'Lotte, I need to talk to you about Adrian.'

After a minute she heard footsteps and the door opened slowly. Lotte Clarke stood inside, pale-faced and red-eyed. She was swamped in a thick cardigan, which she wrapped protectively around herself.

'What do you want?' she demanded.

'I need to talk to you about Adrian. He was—'

'You told the police about me and Adrian, didn't you?' Lotte said, her voice breaking. She dragged a cardigan sleeve across her face. 'You told them I was hiding him.'

'You were. Lotte, I'm so sorry that—'

'Well, I told them who did it,' she snarled.

Emma took half a step back. 'Who?' she asked.

'It was Lydia. She had it in for Adrian from the start. She hated him, always trying to get him sacked just because he was having some problems.' She was breathing heavily. 'Plus he knew she was having an affair and he said he was going to tell her boyfriend if she didn't leave him alone.'

Emma's eyes widened. 'He was going to tell? What did Lydia say?'

'She said she'd kill him if he said anything.' Lotte's words seemed to almost choke her and she wrapped her cardigan more tightly around her thin body. 'And now he's dead. Did you tell her where you were meeting him so she could kill him?' she demanded.

Emma took a slight step backwards. 'What? No, why would I? Why would she have killed him before the opening?'

'Her boyfriend was there,' Lotte snapped. 'She'd been horrible to Adrian earlier in the day on the phone. He told her she'd gone too far this time and if he saw her boyfriend then he was going to tell him everything. That's why she killed him.'

'But it wasn't Adrian,' Emma said quietly.

Lotte sniffed, tears starting in her eyes. 'No, she killed the wrong man. Poor Martin didn't deserve that.'

Emma had opened her mouth to speak when a voice behind her demanded, 'What do you think you're doing?'

Emma whipped around and came face-to-face with Helena. She'd been so intent on Lotte that she hadn't heard the Toyota Hybrid pull onto the driveway. Damn electric cars, she thought.

'I asked what you think you're doing,' Helena snapped, stepping forward.

'I'm talking to Lotte about Adrian Kendall. She knew him and—' Emma began then she stopped short, seeing the ugly expression on Helena's chubby face.

'She knows nothing about that man; she was nowhere near him when he was killed. I told the police the same thing.' Helena pushed roughly past Emma, almost knocking her into the garden, and placed herself in front of Lotte.

'It's because of people like you that my poor Lotte is so stressed and ill,' she said, stepping forward towards Emma, who retreated a few paces.

'Lotte, any time you want to talk—' Emma began but Helena took another step forward and pushed Emma backwards with both hands. Emma fell against the side of the Toyota and only just saved herself. Helena advanced and pushed her further down the drive. This time Emma fell to the ground, landing on her bottom and rolling onto her back. She just managed to protect her head, which was still hurting from the night before.

'You leave my daughter alone,' Helena snarled, standing over Emma as she struggled to her feet. When she was upright, Helena jabbed a finger into Emma's chest. 'Get off my driveway and, if I see you around her again, I'll make you very sorry,' she said, stepping forward again.

Emma quickly backed away and began to walk towards her car. She looked back just in time to see Helena bundling Lotte inside and slamming the front door.

Chapter twenty-three

All it took was a short text message conversation for Emma and Dan to arrange a trip to The Tavern that evening. The Friday night post-work crowd was already beginning to arrive but Emma was able to secure them a corner table where they'd get some privacy. While she waited she fulfilled her crime reporter duties, checking in with the police, fire and ambulance press offices and filing a couple of small stories to the evening news editor. Typing into her phone was difficult as her hands were still a bit wobbly after her encounter with Helena Clarke.

There was a gust of cold air and Dan arrived, unzipping his coat. 'Are you OK?' he asked, hanging his coat on the back of a chair and sliding across it to give her a hug and a kiss.

Emma puffed out her cheeks. 'Only just.'

'That woman is mental,' Dan said, pushing a stray strand of hair behind her ear. Emma kissed him back and held up her hand to show it was still trembling a little. 'You didn't hit your head again, did you?' he asked, anxiously turning her head so he could see the bump from the previous night.

'No, but my neck is aching now from stopping my head hitting the ground,' she said, massaging the back of it.

Dan pointed towards the bar. 'Doctor Sullivan now prescribes a large glass of wine.'

'I like this Doctor Sullivan.' Emma grinned. 'For today I'll stick to lime and soda. I'm feeling a bit queasy.'

Dan peered at her. 'Is it because of your head? Should you go to the hospital?'

Emma shook her head. 'No, I think it's the Helena Effect.'

Dan nodded and Emma watched as he strode across the room. When he came back, he sat down. 'Ed's at the cop shop,' he said. 'The police have just pulled Lydia in again.'

Emma sighed. 'I had a feeling that might happen.'

'Well, they questioned her last time when they thought Adrian was killed,' Dan said. 'It stands to reason they'd want to talk to her again now he is actually dead.'

Emma shook her head. 'No, it's something Lotte told them,' she said, chewing the inside of her mouth and wondering what to tell Dan. He picked up his pint, indicating for her to grab her lime and soda. When she did, he chinked his glass against hers and took a sip.

Then, seeing the expression on her face, he frowned. 'What did Lotte tell them?' he asked.

Emma braced herself. 'Lydia's been seeing someone else,' she said, quietly.

Dan stared at her, his pint hovering between the table and his mouth. 'What?' he demanded loudly. 'How do you know that?'

'She told me. She said they've been going out for the last month and they've kissed a few times.'

'What?!' Dan's voice was almost a squeak and he quickly cleared his throat.

'She said the guy phoned her while she was waiting for Adrian backstage and she stepped away to speak to him. That's why she couldn't have stabbed Martin. The first time she saw him was in the window when he collapsed.'

Dan was staring at her, mouth hanging open. 'Why didn't you say anything?' he asked sharply.

'What? Tell Ed that Lydia was seeing some other guy? He was already furious with me and he'd think I was just stirring,' Emma snapped back. She took a sip of her drink. 'What are you going to do?'

'I have to tell him. I can't see him all day every day and not say anything. It'll kill me and then when he finds out I knew and didn't say anything he'll kill me as well.'

'Dan—'

'Look, I know you think it's none of our business, but could you seriously sit next to Ed all day at work, go for drinks in the evening, knowing what you know and being OK with it?'

Emma sighed. 'No, I guess not.'

'Do you think Lydia will tell him?' Dan asked.

Emma shrugged. 'I don't think she was even planning to tell the police. She might be forced to if the alternative is a murder charge.'

'How is Lydia's love life connected to Adrian Kendall's murder?' Dan asked, taking a gulp of his pint as if his life depended on it. 'Or Martin's murder for that matter?'

'Lotte said that Adrian knew about the affair, for want of a better word, and that he'd told Lydia he would tell Ed if she didn't stop being so horrible to him. I think that's why she was trying to get Tony to sack him. It was nothing to do with being late.'

Dan took a sharp intake of breath. 'Do you think Adrian would do that?'

Emma shrugged. 'I don't know. All Lotte told me was that Lydia and Adrian had rowed at lunchtime on the day of the opening, which Lydia already told us. Ed was at Fenleys on Saturday; he said he was even inside the shop at one point. The police could think that Lydia killed Adrian to stop him telling Ed. The smoking woman from the café said me she heard Lydia threaten to kill Adrian. Maybe it wasn't about him screwing up Christmas.'

'Lydia couldn't have killed Martin, who was supposed to be Adrian, if she was on the phone with this bloke,' Dan said, gripping his pint so tightly Emma was worried he would smash the glass.

Emma nodded. 'We don't know whether Lydia has an alibi for the time when Adrian was killed. He was alive when I found him and he was trying to tell me something. Maybe he was trying to tell me who killed Martin, and stabbed him. Then they whacked me on the head to make sure I couldn't help him,' she said, pausing with her glass halfway to her lips.

Dan nodded. 'And?'

'Well, can you really see Lydia whacking me on the head? The paramedic said Adrian had lost too much blood for me to save him anyway so there was no need to hit me.'

'Maybe she needed to get away and was worried that you would see her?'

Emma winced. 'I dunno, Dan. I really don't know what to think. It's going to come down to whether Lydia has an alibi for the time Adrian was killed.'

'You still think she could have stabbed him?' Dan asked.

'If it was to protect her relationship with Ed ... maybe,' Emma said, turning her glass round and round on its mat.

'She's cheating on him. Surely that suggests the relationship isn't as important to her as we thought.' Dan took an angry gulp of beer and started to choke. Emma patted him on the back as he spluttered. When he was able to breathe again, she picked up her lime and soda.

'Lotte was very quick to put the blame on Lydia, but the fact she told the police about it makes me think she really believes it. She's devastated by what's happened. She's lost someone who seems to have been a good friend, if not more than that.'

'That explains why she knocked over all those glasses,' Dan said, wiping his eyes on his sleeve. 'By blaming Lydia, you don't think she's overreacting and lashing out at just anyone?'

Emma took a sip. 'No, I think she genuinely believes it. I think Tony Cootes does as well. But, the conversation he overheard wasn't Lydia talking to Adrian about protecting a secret, she was talking to the guy on the phone. So we know Tony's evidence is bogus, even if he believes it.'

'Will the police see it that way?' Dan asked, fiddling with a beer mat on the table.

'If Lydia tells them about the phone call, it'll all go away. Then the police will have to get in touch with the guy and we have to hope he tells them the truth.'

'Do you think there's a chance he might lie?' Dan asked, taking a couple of mouthfuls and setting down his glass.

Emma shrugged. 'You'd think he'd be honest if it's to get Lydia off a murder charge, but what if she doesn't have an alibi for when Adrian was stabbed in the park?'

'She must do,' Dan said, 'because it's the middle of the working day. Why would she be in the park? She'd hardly go out for a stroll or a picnic in the park in this weather.'

'I was in the park,' Emma pointed out.

'You'd been invited so—' Dan saw the doubtful expression on

Emma's face. 'What?'

'Maybe Lydia had been invited as well. Maybe Adrian asked both of us to meet him there and he was going to tell me that Lydia killed Martin.'

'You just said Lydia couldn't have killed Martin,' Dan said, looking bewildered.

Emma groaned and put her face in her hands. 'This is so confusing.'

'You think the killer overheard Adrian arranging to meet you?'

Emma shook her head. 'I don't know. He told me that he couldn't talk on the phone but he didn't say where he was. Maybe the killer was nearby?'

Dan shrugged and finished his pint. 'That depends where he was hiding, I suppose. If Lydia didn't do it, then who else had a reason to kill Adrian?'

'There are a few options,' Emma said, taking a sip of lime and soda and wincing as the bubbles tried to go up her nose. 'Tony Cootes. There was definitely something going on between him and Adrian. He tried to stop Adrian from being Santa even though he's always been really popular. He was also very quick to tell me about Lydia arguing with Adrian and saying he thought she might have done it,' Emma said.

'You think he might be covering his own back?' Dan asked, twisting his glass until it was in the centre of his mat.

Emma nodded. 'He said that he went back into the shop to get his phone and overheard Lydia. She was on the phone and walked away from the backstage area to take the call.

'What if he went backstage, waited until she left the area and then snuck in? There was no one else around to see that he didn't do that.'

'He would have had time to put the knife back and then get

back outside before anyone noticed,' Dan said.

'And who would suspect the store manager wandering around and checking a display?' Emma asked. She put her glass down with a thump. 'I need to talk to Tony Cootes again and find out exactly what he was doing the night Martin Kendall died. I also want to know whether he was in the woods yesterday and why he wanted Adrian Kendall dead.'

Chapter twenty-four

When Tony Cootes arrived at the staff entrance of Fenleys on Saturday morning, he found Emma waiting for him. A mixture of irritation and anxiety passed over his face.

'What do you want?' he demanded, a hand poised over the entry keypad.

'We need to talk,' Emma said, shoving her hands into her coat pockets. She'd forgotten her gloves and a bitterly cold wind was whistling down the alleyway to the multi-storey car park.

'I don't need to talk to you about anything,' he snapped, but his posture was that of an animal trying to find an escape from a predator.

'We need to talk about Adrian and why you didn't want him to be Santa this year,' Emma said, taking a step forward.

Tony Cootes's hand clenched several times as if he was trying to get rid of pins and needles. 'I never said—'

'Oh, come on Tony, we both know that you chose someone else first. Why did you change your mind?'

Tony made a growling noise in his throat.

Emma examined him, head tilted to one side. 'Someone asked

you to reconsider, didn't they?' she said slowly, an idea dawning on her. 'I'm right, aren't I?' She paused as Tony's cheeks flushed.

'You don't know what you're talking about,' he blustered. 'I just wanted something different. I...'

He broke off and Emma continued to stare at him, hoping her silence would make him speak.

'Look, I don't know what you're trying to do. There's no scandal here,' Tony continued, speaking very quickly.

Emma rolled her eyes. 'I don't work for a tabloid and I'm not looking for scandal. I'm trying to find out who killed Martin and Adrian Kendall and I want to know why you didn't want him to be Santa.' She sensed a weakening in Tony and pressed on. 'Someone killed two guys who are, to all intents and purposes, nice and respectable people but—'

Tony snorted. 'Adrian wasn't nice,' he said and then stopped abruptly as if he'd said too much.

Emma eyed him. 'What do you mean by that? Was he up to something dodgy with the kids?'

Tony shook his head emphatically. 'No, no, nothing like that. He was...' His voice trailed away and he looked up and down the alley in a furtive manner.

Emma followed his gaze. 'There's no one around, Tony. Why not just tell me?'

His cheeks coloured even more and he tried to turn away to hide his face.

'Look, it's freezing out here,' she said, trying to control her chattering teeth. 'Shall we go and get a coffee?' She pointed back down the alley to the high street.

Tony shook his head. 'I can't. I've got a shop to open.' He took a deep breath and sighed. 'You're not going to go away, are you?' When Emma shook her head, he sighed again. 'Why don't you come in? I can make coffee in my office while I'm sorting out a few things.'

He tapped a number into the keypad and held the door open for her. Emma stepped inside and then followed him upstairs to his office.

Tony indicated the sofa in the corner of his office and then left the room. Emma sat and through the open door she could hear the sounds of Tony pouring water and opening what sounded like a packet of ground coffee. He came back and perched on the edge of his desk.

'It should only be a couple of minutes,' he said, pointing towards the door.

There was silence as Emma waited for him to carry on the conversation, but when he didn't she stepped in.

'So what did Adrian do that was so bad if it didn't involve the children?'

Tony seemed to be thinking quickly, then said, 'I felt he was being over-familiar with some of the younger female members of staff.'

Emma raised her eyebrows. 'Do you just mean Lotte, or were there others?'

'Just Lotte,' Tony said in a low voice.

There was a beeping noise outside the door and he went out to the coffee machine, returning with two mugs of black coffee. 'Do you want milk?' he asked.

Emma shook her head. She did take milk but she had a feeling that might break the mood. 'Why did you think he was over-familiar?' she asked.

Tony walked over and perched on his desk, putting his mug down on the wooden surface. 'I first saw them together a couple of months ago. It seemed like every time I went on the shop floor he was there chatting to her while she was stacking shelves, or whatever. She seemed a bit uncomfortable so I made sure I kept an eye on things.' He paused.

'Did she ever say he was bothering her?' Emma asked.

Tony shifted awkwardly on his desk. 'Never in so many words, although she didn't seem happy about the attention he was giving her. So when he was suggested as Santa, I decided to go with someone else.'

'You wanted to keep him away from her? He could still come in the shop.'

'I could always move her away from him if I needed to. If he was Santa he'd be around more and she'd not be able to get away from him.'

'Why did you give in and let him be Santa?'

Tony sighed. 'Lotte came to me and begged me to use Adrian as usual. She said he was great at being Santa, the kids always loved him; that it would mean so much to her if he could do the job.'

Emma had picked up her mug to take a sip but put it back down without drinking. 'It would mean so much to her? What did she mean by that?'

Tony cradled his mug in both hands. Emma suspected he was buying time. 'I didn't know at the time, then once I'd employed him, things changed between them. She was always happy to see him and then they started meeting for coffee.'

'You don't sound happy about that,' Emma said, an idea popping into her head.

Tony shrugged. 'It was up to her who she went out with.'

'You were jealous, weren't you? You like Lotte?' Tony flushed red and Emma knew she'd hit the nail on the head. 'That's the real reason you wanted to keep them apart.'

He rubbed his forehead. 'So what if it was? He was about twenty years older than her. It was all wrong. She should have...'

'Been with someone like you? You're not much closer to her age.'

'Closer than him,' Tony said, slightly sulkily. He puffed out his cheeks. 'Then before long I had Lydia clamouring in my ear to get rid of him for some reason. She said he was being unreliable.'

'What did she mean by that?'

Tony sighed and looked down at the floor. 'We have one photoshoot for the promo materials, adverts, posters, that kind of thing. He cut that one really fine and we thought we were going to have to reschedule. He made it to the children's ward visit just in time as well. He *was* late for the dress rehearsal and kept everyone hanging around. Even though it was so close to the opening, Lydia was insistent that I had to tell him I'd replace him if he was late again.'

Emma took a sip of coffee and put down her mug. 'Were you going to sack him on the night of the opening?' she asked.

Tony looked at her from under his eyelashes but before he could answer, the outer door to the office flew open and a cheery voice called, 'Morning, Tony.'

Emma winced, recognising Lydia's voice, and got to her feet.

'I need to talk to you about—' Lydia was saying as she marched into the office. Seeing Emma, she stopped short. 'Sorry, am I interrupting?' she asked, looking at Tony.

He shook his head and downed the rest of his coffee. 'No, we were just finished,' he said, putting his mug down on his desk. He stood up and Emma recognised that she wasn't going to get anything more from him with Lydia staring at her, arms folded.

She got to her feet. 'Thanks for your help with that, Tony,' she said. The man's eyes were pleading with her not to mention their conversation. She turned away and Lydia stepped aside to let Emma walk past her into the outer office. Tony followed and led Emma through the door into the shop.

She turned back to face him. 'I now know you had motive to get rid of Adrian and—'

'What?' Tony spluttered. 'You think I'd kill him because of...'

Emma shrugged. 'I think you're in love with Lotte and you were jealous of her relationship with Adrian. Murder has been committed over less than that. You also had access to the murder weapon and the opportunity to use it while you were backstage, allegedly looking for your phone.' She paused. 'I don't care about your jealousy and secret keeping. But I *am* going to find out who killed Adrian and Martin. Their friends deserve to know what happened to them and why.'

She turned and walked away.

Chapter twenty-five

'Do you still think Tony Cootes would have killed Adrian?' Dan shouted through from the kitchen. He and Emma had decided to have a Saturday night in at his and Ed's flat, while Ed was out with Lydia.

Emma got up from the sofa and went to stand in the kitchen doorway, watching him potter about, putting a shepherd's pie ready meal into the oven. She sighed. 'I don't see why not. He was in love with Lotte and he was backstage before the opening when Martin was wearing the Santa costume.'

'Is that enough?' Dan asked, turning to face her and leaning against the work surface.

Emma nodded. 'I'm sure he's been in love with Lotte for months and then along comes this other guy and sweeps her out from under him. So to speak,' she added as Dan sniggered. 'Whichever way you look at it, he had means, motive and opportunity.'

'It's the timing I don't get,' Dan said, picking up his beer bottle and taking a swig. 'Why do it at the opening?'

Emma frowned. 'That's where I'm stumped too. Unless

something wound him up on the day, he saw red and—' she made a stabbing motion with her hand.

'That would explain the murder weapon being so close to hand,' Dan said, pointing at her with the neck of his beer bottle.

'Picking up the knife from the other side of the shop shows premeditation,' Emma said, taking a sip of water. 'He'd have had to go over there deliberately, get the knife and come back.'

Dan sighed. 'If he stabbed Santa, and Santa collapsed in the backstage area, what was he going to do? Put the suit on himself? Surely that would have looked a bit odd.'

Emma frowned. 'Not necessarily, because he could have just lied and said Adrian was late. What's more intriguing is what he would have done with the body if Martin hadn't staggered away into the window display.'

Dan took a swig of his beer. 'I suppose he could have dumped it somewhere out of sight and then someone could have found it later. Then after all that, he found out he'd killed the wrong bloke.' He put down his beer bottle and opened the oven door to check the progress of the pie. He closed it again, and turned back to Emma. 'I bet that was a shock.'

Emma nodded. 'He said he didn't realise that it wasn't Adrian when he saw him dead in the window.'

'I suppose one man in a big bushy beard looks much like another.' Dan paused when he saw Emma frown. 'What?'

'Is it even possible that he *didn't* know it wasn't Adrian? He was right up close to Martin when he pushed Lydia away. Would you not pull the beard off and try to do first aid or something?'

Dan shrugged. 'Maybe he realised Santa was dead and he wanted to keep people away from the scene?'

'That's what Lydia said – preserving the crime scene.'

'Did he say anything about where he was when Adrian was

killed?' Dan asked.

Emma shook her head. 'I didn't get that far. Lydia barged in and Tony couldn't get me out of the office quick enough.'

'Did anyone else see Tony backstage when he claims he was?' Dan asked.

Emma shook her head. 'I've no idea. The police don't seem to have anyone, and Lydia said she didn't see anyone but she was away from the area. The only person who could tell us is Martin and he can't say anything.' She took a sip of water. 'This feels like one enormous knot. I know that if I pull one thread it'll all come undone, but I'm damned if I can work out which one.'

Dan leaned against the cupboard. 'If it's not Lydia and possibly not Tony, who does that leave us with?' he asked.

Emma frowned and rubbed her chin. 'What about Helena?' she asked.

Dan stared at her. 'Lotte's mum? You think she killed Martin and Adrian?'

Emma nodded. 'She's really possessive of Lotte, and Tony told me that she picks Lotte up from work so she can't go out anywhere—'

'Hang on,' Dan interrupted, 'if Helena picks her up from work, then how could Lotte go to Adrian's flat that day when you saw her? Where was Helena?'

Emma frowned. 'Lotte must have given her the slip somehow. But, if Helena found out that Lotte was seeing Adrian, she wouldn't be happy.'

'Enough to kill him?' Dan asked, looking dubious.

'We know she's a bit unhinged,' Emma said, rubbing her lower back. 'She pushed me over just for talking to Lotte.'

Dan puffed out his cheeks. 'I suppose she could have seen Adrian and Lotte together if she was picking her up from work.

It would explain why she was trying to stop Lotte working at Fenleys.'

Emma took another sip of water. 'None of this explains why Adrian was being so unreliable this year. Tony said he was late for the promo photo shoot, he almost missed the children's ward visit; what was he doing?'

'Spending all his time with Lotte?' Dan asked.

Emma walked over to the dining table and put her glass down. She tugged at the end of her curly red ponytail. 'Maybe that's true. They would have had to hide their relationship from Helena so maybe that needed a lot of sneaking around.'

'There's one other thing,' Dan said. 'Something was different at the opening on Saturday.'

'Different how?'

'Well, this time, Martin was on standby to step in.'

Emma frowned. 'You mean that Adrian already knew there was a chance he wouldn't make it in time?'

'Exactly. He must have known that Martin in the suit and beard could pass for him and he wouldn't spoil opening night.'

Emma scratched her head. 'What could Adrian have been doing that would be worth being late for the big moment, the start of the Christmas season, which by all accounts he loved?'

The oven timer began to beep.

'Well,' Dan said, straightening up and grabbing the oven gloves, 'dinner is served so let's park this for now and come back to it once we've eaten.'

***

Emma and Dan were just setting the kitchen to rights after dinner when her phone rang.

Dan groaned as he washed a plate and propped it up on the draining board. 'That had better not be work,' he said. 'I was really looking forward to watching that film in one go without having to stop every ten minutes for you to check your phone.'

Emma flicked him with the tea towel she was using to dry up and walked into the sitting room. She picked up her phone from the coffee table and answered.

'Hello, is that Emma Fletcher?' a well-spoken voice asked.

'Yes, speaking.'

'It's Oliver Gateby here.'

'Oh, hello, how are you?' Emma asked, tucking her phone under her chin and wiping her hands on the tea towel.

The man sighed. 'As well as can be expected, is that the phrase?' Emma smiled sadly. 'Yes, I believe it is. What can I do for you?'

'Sorry to bother you in the evening, I was just going to leave a message. Something about Adrian has just come to mind.'

Emma sat down on the sofa, dumped the towel and grabbed her notebook from her bag, which lay on the floor. 'Go ahead,' she said, tapping her phone to put it on speaker and clicking out the point of her pen.

'I've been at Martin's starting to clear out some stuff.' She heard him take a shuddering breath. 'While I was doing that, I found some theatre programmes from shows Adrian had been in.'

Emma frowned. 'I thought Adrian and Martin weren't on speaking terms while he was in London,' she said.

'Oh, they're not from the London days,' Oliver said. 'They're stuff he's done since he's been back.' He gave a little laugh. 'I think Martin has been to every one of them. Making up for the lost years, I think. I went along to one and it was rather good.'

'Is it a professional company?' Emma asked.

'Oh yes. Adrian was much too good to be in am-dram, in my opinion. He was involved with the Apollo Theatre Company, based at the Octavian Playhouse in Allensbury. You know it?'

'Yes, our arts reporter covers all the shows there.'

Oliver paused and she thought she could hear him taking a drink. 'As well as being in the cast of most of their plays, he worked with their youth theatre group. He had them trained to a very professional standard. I've seen a lot of plays on London stages that weren't as good as that.'

'I wonder what his secret was,' Emma said.

'Oh, definitely practice. I know he spent hours rehearsing the cast; I've no doubt they could all run the show backwards by opening night.'

'Was it only during the evenings?' Emma asked, an idea forming in her head.

'They worked at all hours, from what Martin said,' Oliver replied. 'I think some of the kids were at the drama school or one of the other local colleges. They have funny hours for lectures and suchlike so they often rehearsed during the day. He worked them hard, but it definitely paid off. They could have taken the show on national tour and it would have fitted in with any professional company.'

Emma stared off into the distance. Was that why Adrian had been late to the Fenleys photo call and the hospital visit? He was putting the student actors first?

Oliver's next words brought her attention back sharply. 'I believe he greatly regretted that he'd never had a family of his own. There had been some lost woman in his past who I don't think he'd ever got over. Neither he nor Martin really spoke about her in front of me.'

'A woman?' Emma asked. She looked up and saw Dan leaning in the doorway, totally focused on Oliver's voice.

'I don't know much about it – they didn't talk family business in front of me – but I do know that Adrian was working every hour he could to get money for this woman. Martin was worried about him and tried to lend him money; Adrian wouldn't have it.'

'He wouldn't take a penny from Martin?' Emma asked.

'No, I overheard a conversation once where Adrian said it was his problem so he needed to fix it. He'd left her in that situation, and it was his responsibility to get her out.'

Emma sat back against the sofa cushions and Dan took a step forward into the room. 'Martin didn't tell you anything about the woman? Anything at all?' Emma asked.

She could hear Oliver take another drink. 'I know Martin was worried about what Adrian was doing; he said someone was going to get hurt.' He stopped speaking and Emma heard him sniff loudly. 'I guess he was right.'

Chapter twenty-six

Andrew Burgess, the Apollo Theatre Company's manager, looked nervous when he met Emma in the reception area of the theatre on Monday afternoon.

'I think I can guess why you're here,' he said, his smile not quite reaching his eyes.

'I'm writing a tribute piece about Adrian Kendall,' Emma said, 'and I'm getting quotes from people who knew him.'

Andrew nodded. 'I'm happy to speak to you but I need to set up for the next class while we talk. Is that OK?' When Emma nodded, he led the way along a corridor to a brightly lit studio. 'Adrian's class will be arriving soon and I want to have a space for them to settle down and talk. It's the first time they've been together since it ... since it happened.' His voice trailed off.

Emma nodded, feeling a coldness again, remembering her attempts to save Adrian. 'They're coming to rehearse even though he's gone?' she asked.

Andrew shook his head. 'There won't be any rehearsing today. They're all so shaken up. Well, they thought he'd died at the opening, which was bad enough. Then to learn he's alive and have him killed again ... it's a lot to take in.' He walked across the room and began to take chairs from a stack in the corner and place them in the middle of the room. 'They're mature for seventeen-year-olds but I don't think anyone would be surprised that they're completely blindsided by this.'

Emma put her handbag down on the floor and helped him with the chairs. He smiled gratefully.

'What will they be doing today?' Emma asked, putting a chair next to another, starting to form a semi-circle.

'My sister specialises in grief counselling,' Andrew said, adding another chair. 'She's coming down later to talk to them.'

Emma nodded. 'That's certainly a good idea,' she said, placing another chair next to his.

Andrew did a quick count of the chairs. 'That should be enough,' he said, indicating for Emma to sit down. He sat a couple of seats away from her. 'So, how can I help?'

'I'm trying to get some background on Adrian,' she said, 'and I spoke to a friend of his who told me Adrian was working for the company.'

Andrew nodded. 'When he first auditioned to join the company as an actor, I almost snatched his arm off. I would have hired him without an audition but it's procedure. To get someone so talented was a real coup. Then, a few months ago, when he said he'd work with the kids for a bit of extra cash, I was delighted. They love him and they respect his track record. He's what they aspire to be.'

'His agent said he loved working with young people.'

Andrew nodded. 'And he was really good at it, I mean *really* good. He would have made a brilliant teacher if he hadn't been an actor. He made it easy for them to see what he wanted them to do.'

'Had he been working here for long?' Emma asked.

'Ever since he came back to Allensbury,' Andrew said. 'Like I say, we were holding auditions at the time and I jumped at the chance.'

'You knew about his gig with Fenleys?' she asked.

Andrew nodded. 'Of course.'

'How did that fit with his theatre company activities?'

Andrew frowned. 'It was only for a few hours a day and he managed to make it work.'

'Was he ever late for rehearsals or performances?' Emma asked, scribbling notes.

'He's come close with a few rehearsals recently,' Andrew started, then paused. 'Actually, now you mention it, I nearly had to take one of his sessions a week or so ago because he was nearly ten minutes late. He was embarrassed and apologetic, and I gave him the benefit of the doubt as it was only the once.'

Emma frowned at her notebook as she continued to scribble. So it wasn't just Fenleys Adrian was late for. 'Did he say where he'd been?'

Andrew shook his head. 'He just said he had some business to take care of. The kids teased him about it, asking if he'd been making toys in his workshop or tuning up the sleigh and lost track of time. That made him laugh. They all went along to support him on the night.' Andrew's mouth turned down again.

Emma was silent for a moment, the coldness returning, imagining how it would have felt for Adrian's students. 'What time did he leave the theatre on Saturday?' she asked.

'That's what's been bothering me,' Andrew said. 'Our session packed up about an hour before he was due to be at Fenleys. He was a bit on edge, to be honest. The kids wanted to walk down to the shop with him. He said he had stuff to do and would see us afterwards for a glass of sherry and a mince pie.' He smiled sadly. 'One of the kids even stopped off at the shop on the way to get mince pies as a joke. It didn't feel right to eat them after what happened to Adrian. They're in my cupboard at home.'

'What happened when you found out it wasn't Adrian in the Santa suit?' Emma asked, looking up from her notebook.

He sighed. 'I couldn't quite believe what I was reading and I tried to call him immediately. He must have been in shock, having lost his brother. I wanted to comfort him but there was no answer. Then two days later he called me back. I was in a class so my phone was off, and he left a message.' He pulled his phone from the pocket of his jeans. 'Here, I'll play it for you.' He dialled a number and then put it on speaker phone. A voice Emma immediately recognised spoke.

'Andrew? I'm sorry I've not been in touch. Well, I'm sure you know why by now. I think it was supposed to be me and I'm scared.' The voice choked slightly and Emma got a shiver down her spine. Listening to a dead man speak was unreal. 'Please, please, can you call me back as soon as you get this? I need your help but I can't come to the theatre. I need to hide. Call me, please.' There was a click as the message ended and Andrew hung up the phone. There was silence in the room as Emma tried to take in what she'd heard.

'It was horrible to turn my phone back on and hear that,' Andrew said. 'I tried to call him straightaway and there was no answer.' He rubbed a hand across his face. 'I just keep thinking of him dying alone and—'

'He wasn't alone,' Emma cut in, feeling a lump in her throat. 'I found him. I tried to stop the bleeding but there was too much and—' Her voice cracked and she thought she was going to cry.

Andrew leaned over and put a hand on hers. 'I'm sure you did everything you could to help.'

Emma nodded, her throat aching with the effort of not crying. She sniffed and looked back at Andrew.

He looked close to tears himself. 'If only I'd answered the phone when he called, if only...' Andrew's voice trailed away.

'Don't think like that, it'll drive you mad,' Emma said, trying to sound reassuring. She took a deep breath, hoping she'd got herself under control. 'Did he have any particular friends, a girlfriend maybe?'

Andrew shook his head. 'No one he spoke of, although I did once hear him on the phone and he called the other person "sweetheart". He never told me who it was and I didn't ask. He was a private guy.' Then he frowned. 'Although, there was another call, and he certainly wasn't calling that person "sweetheart".'

'How do you mean?' Emma asked, almost holding her breath.

'Well, it sounded like a man's voice. He was shouting, that's how I could hear. Adrian had to hold the phone away from his ear and he said, "don't you threaten me, you know you have to do this; you signed a contract."'

'You couldn't hear who was on the other end?'

'No, but Adrian said, "Tony, you know she's on my side; they all are. You can't do this." The other guy shouted a bit more and then hung up.'

'How did Adrian seem?'

'A little unsettled in the way you would be after a row with someone. Then he smiled as he was putting away his phone. Like he'd won the argument and was a bit pleased with himself.'

Emma opened her mouth to speak but at that moment the door flew open and a group of six teenagers filed in. They stopped short when they saw Andrew and Emma.

'Shall we come back?' the one at the front asked, pointing a thumb back over his shoulder. Andrew looked at Emma.

She shook her head and got to her feet. 'No, thank you, I think I've got everything I need. Thanks for your time.'

As she left the theatre, she pulled out her mobile phone and dialled the number she wanted. When Dan answered, she asked, 'Where are you? I need to talk to you.'

Chapter twenty-seven

Emma battled a flood of tears as she walked back to the *Allensbury Post*'s building. Dan was waiting by the front steps, looking very serious. He stepped forward and held out his arms to her. She walked straight into them, tears starting to flow. Dan squeezed her and whispered comforting noises in her ear. It was a couple of minutes before Emma could regain control of herself. Then she pulled away and dug a hand into her bag for a packet of tissues. She pulled one out and started to wipe her face. She pointed to the damp patch on Dan's shoulder.

'Sorry, I've wet your jacket,' she sniffed.

He glanced down at it and smiled at her. 'Your tears and snotty nose are welcome on my jacket anytime, you know that.' He ran a hand down her arm and gripped her hand. 'Come on, let's get you home for a cuppa,' he said, tugging at her hand. She let him pull her along, still wiping her face with the tissue in her other hand.

'So it wasn't just Fenleys that Adrian was being late for?' Dan asked. 'And he didn't tell the theatre guy where he'd been?'

Emma shook her head. 'No. Andrew Burgess said he was a

private guy and didn't give much away.' She took a deep breath and exhaled heavily. 'I'm more intrigued by the phone call he got.'

'The phone call from Tony?' Dan asked.

'It has to be Tony Cootes, right?'

Dan shrugged. He stopped at the pedestrian crossing at the bottom of the hill and pressed the button. 'It's not exactly an uncommon name,' he said, 'although I'd say it gives you good grounds to go and ask Tony Cootes why he was threatening Adrian.'

'Threatening to sack him?' Emma asked.

Dan frowned. 'Or were they talking about Lotte?'

Emma nodded. 'I'm guessing the "she" they were talking about was Lotte. My only problem is why he would sack Adrian and risk ruining the opening?'

The pedestrian crossing began to beep and they crossed the road.

Dan sighed. 'Like we said last night, what if he had a replacement waiting in the wings? He had a back-up Santa and was going to bring him in instead.'

Emma stopped suddenly and stared at him. Dan walked a few more steps before he realised she wasn't beside him.

'What's the matter?' he asked.

'Could he have been the one who made Adrian late on the night? To give him grounds to sack him once the opening was done?'

Dan walked back and tugged her arm to make her start walking again.

'How would he make Adrian late? What could he have sent him to do? And why would he then go backstage and kill him?' Dan asked, as they turned the corner into Emma's street.

'I think Adrian had done something that made him angry,' Emma said.

'What, like turn up on time?' Dan asked, as they arrived outside the door and Emma pulled out her keys.

'No, I think he'd done something more serious,' Emma said, 'that it had happened on the day of the opening. Tony was so upset by it that he lashed out without thinking about what would happen if Adrian didn't do the opening.'

'And like the police said, Adrian, who was really Martin, staggered into the window to escape him.'

Emma nodded as she took off her coat and shoes in the small hallway. 'By that point Tony couldn't do anything because the opening was about to happen and he couldn't stop it. He also had to get away and get rid of the knife before Lydia turned up. Maybe he heard her coming back from her phone call.'

Dan hung up his coat and followed her into the living room. 'And you have that look in your eyes that suggests you have a theory about why Tony did it,' he said, sitting down on the sofa.

Emma headed towards the kitchen. 'Drink?' she asked from the doorway.

'Yes, please.' Dan watched as she went into the kitchen. He heard sounds of water being poured into the kettle and it being switched on.

Emma returned clutching a packet of custard creams.

Seeing the smug smile on her face, Dan looked at her expectantly as she sat down. 'You're not going to tell me, are you?'

Emma grinned. 'Nope, I want to test it out before I say anything.'

'You know I have ways of making you talk,' Dan said, taking the biscuits from her hand and putting them on the table. He pounced on her and started to tickle her. Emma squealed and soon the tickling turned to kissing, and the theory went right out of her head.

Chapter twenty-eight

On Tuesday morning, Emma marched into Fenleys still trying to think of a pretext to get into Tony Cootes's office for a private chat. Instead she encountered Lydia.

'How's it going?' she asked.

Lydia puffed out her cheeks. 'The police interviewed me again after Adrian was killed.'

Emma nodded. 'I wondered if they might.'

'Anyway, I had a good alibi. I was in a meeting with ten other people so there was no way I was in the park.'

Emma smiled. 'That must be a relief.' Then she took a deep breath and looked at Lydia. 'Did the police speak to Will?' she asked, checking around to make sure no one could overhear them.

Lydia flushed and nodded. 'He told them that we'd been speaking at the time of Martin's murder.'

'Are you going to tell Ed about him?'

Lydia nodded again. 'I'm going to have to. I told Will I can't see him anymore.'

Emma winced. 'How did he take it?'

'Not well. He's threatening to tell Ed now, so I'm going to have to get to him first. Ed, that is.'

'You also need to get to Ed before Dan does,' Emma said wincing. When Lydia scowled at her, Emma added, 'I didn't mean to tell him. He wanted to know why you'd been pulled in for questioning. I had to explain that Lotte had told the police about the affair. He'd have found out anyway because Will was your alibi for Martin's murder.'

Lydia sighed heavily. 'Ed's going to be crushed,' she said, the corners of her mouth pulling down.

Emma sighed and puffed out her cheeks. 'I think that's a risk you're going to have to take. Better that he hears it from you than someone else.'

Lydia was silent for a moment. Then she asked, 'What are you doing here anyway?'

'I need to speak to Tony,' Emma said, awkwardly.

'Why?' Lydia asked quietly, leaning towards Emma.

In a low voice, Emma said, 'I think *he* killed Martin and Adrian.' Lydia stared at her. 'Was he in the meeting with you when Adrian was killed?' she asked.

Lydia frowned. 'He was supposed to be,' she said, 'but he cancelled at the last minute and I had to lead it.' She stopped speaking and stared at Emma. 'You think he was in the park stabbing Adrian?' she asked in a whisper.

Emma nodded urgently. 'Yes, and I think someone else could be in danger if I don't speak to him now.'

Lydia grabbed the radio that was clipped to her waistband. She clicked a button and spoke into it.

'Tony, it's Lydia. I'm on the shop floor and I think there's a crack in one of the front windows. Can you come now?' The radio crackled and Tony's voice asked if she was sure. 'Yes, and

I know the glass is toughened. That's why I'm so worried.' She paused. Then Tony agreed to come and Lydia smiled at Emma. 'Wait outside, I'll bring him to you.'

Emma scooted outside and hid in the smokers' alley. She was worried that Lydia might help Tony to escape but she soon heard voices.

'It's along here, Tony, just here,' she could hear Lydia saying. Then before Tony Cootes could react, Lydia had bundled him into the alley. Emma moved so that she and Lydia were both blocking his exit.

Tony cringed away. 'What do you want?' he asked, his voice shaking.

'You threatened Adrian,' Emma said, 'a few days before he died. Were you threatening to sack him? Or were you threatening him with worse?' When Tony didn't speak, Emma continued. 'Someone overheard the call. Adrian telling you that she was on his side, they were all on his side?'

Tony's eyes widened. 'Who told you that?' he asked.

'That's not important. You wanted Adrian gone, because of his relationship with Lotte. That meant *you* couldn't have a relationship with her.'

Lydia gasped and Emma raised a hand to silence her question.

'You were going to sack him after the opening, weren't you?' Emma asked. 'You already had a new Santa set up to take over?' Lydia was staring at Emma open-mouthed. Tony stayed stubbornly silent, glaring at Emma.

'Then on the day of the opening he did something you couldn't forgive, something that made you so angry that you went to the backstage area before the show,' Emma said.

Tony stared at her. 'How do you know that?'

'That's not important. What did he do?' Emma demanded.

Tony cleared his throat. 'I saw Lotte at lunchtime and she was really upset. She showed me bruises on her arms, as if someone had grabbed her hard.' He put out his hands and demonstrated grabbing and shaking. 'I thought at first she meant that it was her mum. Helena has done that before.' He winced. 'She said it was Adrian. She'd been trying to walk away from him and he'd tried to stop her.'

Emma raised her eyebrows. 'And instead you were going to stop *him*?' she asked.

Tony nodded. 'I had to protect her.'

'And you waited 'til he was alone backstage and stabbed him?' Emma asked.

Tony stared at her. 'What? What are you talking about?'

'You were backstage, you told me that. You said you went looking for your phone. Lydia was out of sight taking a phone call. You had time and you had access to the murder weapon.'

Tony looked outraged. 'No, I didn't kill him!' he shouted.

Emma took a step forward. 'It must have been tough finding out that you'd killed the wrong man,' she said. 'When did you realise? When the body was found or when the police told you?'

'I didn't kill him,' Tony insisted. 'You were right that I went backstage to tell Adrian he was fired after that night. I'd already been in touch with another agency for a replacement.' He took a deep shuddering breath. 'I genuinely didn't realise when we found him dead that it wasn't Adrian. I didn't know he had a brother either.' He took a deep breath. 'I didn't even get into the backstage area. Someone called on my radio to say I was needed.' He held up the radio in his hand.

'Who? Who called you?' Lydia demanded.

'Reenie. She said there was a problem at the front of the store and I had to come and help.' Tony was looking urgently from one to the other.

'Why did you skip that meeting on the day Adrian died?' Lydia asked, crossing her arms.

Tony sighed and put his face in his hands. 'Lotte asked to meet me,' he said, his voice muffled. 'She said she needed to talk. She was on a day off so I sneaked out and got coffees for us. Then she was really late.'

'What did she want?' Emma asked.

'She was worried about Adrian. She'd been helping him to hide but he'd gone off somewhere and she didn't know where he was. She said she'd gone to find Helena at work and she'd disappeared as well. She was worried that Helena had found out about them.'

Emma and Lydia exchanged a look.

'What did she want you to do?' Emma asked.

Tony shook his head. 'I never found out. She got a call on her mobile and said she had to dash off.'

'Who was on the phone?' Lydia demanded.

'I don't know. She didn't say and I didn't see the screen.'

Emma was frowning. 'Have you seen Lotte since Adrian died?'

Tony shook his head. 'No, she's been off sick. I think Helena has been keeping her at home. She never wanted Lotte to work here anyway. Didn't like her having a life.'

Lydia was looking at Emma, who was thinking quickly.

When Emma didn't speak, Tony stepped forward. 'I have to get back inside,' he said in a voice that was shaking slightly, whether from emotion or cold, Emma wasn't sure.

She stepped aside without speaking and let him walk past her. He hurried away and into the store.

Lydia shook Emma's arm. 'Is that it?' she demanded.

Emma nodded slowly, staring off into the distance. 'That was a lot to take in,' she said. Then she looked straight at Lydia. 'We need to find Reenie and see what she can tell us about opening night.'

***

Lydia led the way across the shop floor, looking left and right.

'This is the problem, she tends to move around. I never know where she's going to be.' Then she said, 'Aha,' and pointed to the ginger-haired woman stacking a shelf of glasses in the homewares aisle.

'Repairing Lotte's handiwork?' Emma muttered under her breath as Lydia led the way towards Reenie.

Lydia laughed. 'No, we've had a real run on glasses. People preparing for big Christmas dinners.' As they approached, Lydia called, 'Hi, Reenie.'

The woman looked up and smiled. She wiped her hands on a cloth that was slung across the trolley full of boxes of glasses.

'Hello, lovie, how are you?' she asked Lydia.

Lydia smiled. 'Busy as ever, I'm afraid.'

The woman chuckled. 'Always rushing around, this one,' she said to Emma, poking Lydia gently on the arm. Then she peered at Emma. 'Are you new? You look familiar.'

'No, this is my friend Emma,' Lydia said quickly. 'Reenie, I wanted to ask you, on Saturday at the window opening—'

'Oh, that was such a shock,' the woman cut in. 'Poor man. I was so glad it wasn't Adrian, then, of course...' She trailed off, clearly thinking that Adrian had only had a short period of reprieve.

'When we were about to do the opening, did you call Tony to the front of the shop?' Lydia asked.

'He said there was some problem,' Emma put in.

Reenie nodded. 'Yes, some poor little love had fallen over. So excited, they were. We needed the first aid kit, so I called Tony. She was crying a lot so I didn't want to leave the family alone. It didn't seem right,' she said, pursing her lips.

'Did Tony arrive quickly?' Emma asked.

Reenie thought for a moment. 'Yes, he came hurrying over with a first aid kit from behind one of the tills. All it took was a little plaster and she was all smiles again.'

Emma frowned.

Lydia smiled. 'Thanks, Reenie. That was really helpful.' The woman beamed and half-turned to check the glasses in her trolley.

'What are you thinking?' Lydia asked.

Emma rubbed her nose. 'Just because he got the first aid kit quickly doesn't mean he didn't have enough time to kill Martin, drop off the knife and get to the front door.' She paused. 'Was Lotte at the opening?' she asked.

Lydia frowned. 'Now you mention it, I don't remember seeing her. She was working earlier in the day but I was rushing about so much, I wasn't really noticing who was there.'

'Are you talking about Lotte Clarke?' Reenie asked. Lydia and Emma turned to look at her.

'Yes,' Emma said, intrigued to see what Reenie had to say about her.

'Poor little love,' the woman said. 'She has a tough time with her mother from what I've heard.'

'I think everyone has heard that,' Emma said. 'Do you know Lotte's mum?'

Reenie pursed her lips and nodded. 'Not personally but I've known of her for a long time.'

Emma frowned. 'How do you mean?'

'My daughter went to school with her. She said she was always a bit weird, obsessive. Says a lot about how she is now.' The woman shook her head. 'Poor Lotte. At least she had Adrian to cheer her up.'

Emma went very still. She was sending Lydia telepathic messages not to say a word.

'I often saw them giggling together, buying each other coffees and suchlike,' the woman said with a fond smile. 'I've never seen Lotte look so happy. Or Adrian, for that matter, and I've worked with him for years.'

'Did you ever see them hugging?' Emma asked.

The woman thought for a moment. 'Now you mention it, yes, I did see them a couple of times. I was quite surprised because I didn't think Adrian would behave like that towards a younger girl.' She gave a little look over each shoulder as if checking for eavesdroppers and then leaned in. Emma and Lydia leaned in too. 'He was having woman trouble so maybe he was confiding in Lotte.'

'Woman trouble?' Lydia whispered. 'Was he seeing someone?'

'I don't know, sweetheart,' the woman continued. 'All I overheard was him having a proper shouting match with a woman, last week sometime it was. It caught my ear because he's usually such a polite man. He was giving as good as he got.'

'Where was this?' Lydia asked.

'Out the back in the alley that leads to the car park,' the woman replied, pointing over her shoulder and clearly relishing her audience.

'What were they saying?' Emma asked.

'She was shouting, "I can't believe you're doing this to me," and he said, "We can make this work, you just need to give me time to—" then she started shouting, something about he should have thought about that before.' Reenie frowned. 'Then Adrian said he had every right to do what he was doing.'

'What *was* he doing?' Lydia asked, eyes fixed on Reenie.

The woman shook her head. 'I don't know, at that point she burst into tears and stormed off.'

'Did he follow her?' Emma asked.

Reenie shrugged. 'I don't know, dearie, I couldn't see outside. I could just hear them.'

Emma stared at Lydia.

Lydia turned to Reenie. 'Did you recognise the voice?' she asked quietly.

The older woman shook her head. 'No, dearie. She didn't sound familiar. I assumed this was the woman he'd been having trouble with.'

Emma raised her eyebrows. 'What makes you think that?'

'Oh, sweetheart, only lovers can argue the way these two were. Even if they're not lovers anymore. Although—'

At that moment a customer appeared and Reenie immediately stopped talking and a customer-service smile spread across her face.

As she bustled away, Emma and Lydia exchanged a look.

'Who was he arguing with?' Emma asked, scratching her head.

'It can't have been Lotte,' Lydia said, 'or Reenie would have recognised her voice.'

'Helena?'

Lydia snorted. 'I don't think they even knew each other.' She rubbed her nose. 'Either way, we need to find this woman and see who Adrian was dating.'

***

Emma was in the doorway of Fenleys heading out into the high street when a woman's voice called, 'Hey, wait.' She turned to see a slim blonde with a poker-straight ponytail hurrying after her, pulling on a winter coat.

'You were asking about Lotte,' the woman said.

Emma nodded. 'You know her?'

'We're friends. Well, as much as her mum would ever allow. I'm Sally.'

Emma introduced herself. 'Helena doesn't like her having friends?'

The blonde shook her ponytail. 'We've had to keep it a secret.' She looked around. 'Not here. I'm on my break now. Can I buy you a coffee?' Emma nodded and followed her out of the shop and into the Italian café.

Once they had coffees, and Sally had an enormous bacon sandwich in front of her, they sat at a small corner table for two.

'I hope you don't mind,' Sally said, indicating the sandwich. 'I missed breakfast.'

Emma nodded and blew on her coffee, watching Sally take an enthusiastic bite. When she had finished chewing, Emma asked, 'How long have you known Lotte?'

Sally wiped her mouth and fingers on a napkin. 'We were friends at school and college, but Helena doesn't know that we're still in touch. She's really funny about Lotte staying out of the house. Almost as if she thinks Lotte will run away.'

'Would she?' Emma asked, sipping at her coffee and finding it still too hot to drink.

Sally considered for a moment. 'Recently I've felt like it was more likely. Lotte was...' she paused '...acting a bit funny. She gave me some money to look after for her.'

'How much?'

'About two hundred pounds, in cash.'

Emma raised her eyebrows. 'I didn't realise Fenleys paid so well,' she said.

Sally snorted. 'It doesn't; that's why I was so surprised she had so much to spare.' She took another bite of sandwich and chewed.

'Did she tell you where it came from?' Emma asked.

Sally shook her head. 'I asked, but she was really cagey. Just asked me to keep it safe until she needed it. It's hidden in my underwear drawer at home. I don't want anyone asking questions about it. If I put it in the bank I'm sure I'd have accidentally spend it on God knows what. Probably books,' she said with a chuckle.

Emma sipped at her coffee. 'What did you want to tell me?' she asked.

Sally fiddled with a napkin. 'What that woman was telling you ... Lotte isn't that downtrodden, at least not anymore.'

Emma frowned. 'What do you mean?'

'She's up to something – she won't tell me what,' Sally said, sipping her coffee.

'How do you mean?'

'That money; she wouldn't tell me where it came from and I got the impression she was trying to hide it by giving it to me.'

'Who from?'

'Helena,' Sally said. 'She checks Lotte's bank account and if she found extra money in there she would have flipped and made Lotte tell her where it came from.'

'Where do you think she got it?'

Sally took a bite of her sandwich and chewed. She swallowed and wiped her mouth and fingers. Emma felt like it was delaying tactic.

'She's been very friendly with Adrian Kendall recently,' Sally said, once her fingers were fully clean.

'You think it was from him?' Emma asked, feeling her heart starting to beat faster.

Sally shrugged. 'They have been getting very cosy lately.'

'How long have they known each other?' Emma asked, twisting her cup in its saucer.

Sally thought for a moment. 'About six months, I think. I only work here part time because I'm at university in Tildon. I always saw him hanging around though.'

'He might have just been doing some shopping?'

Sally laughed. 'I never saw him buy anything. He just seemed to come in to see Lotte. He'd go and chat to her when she was stacking shelves or whatever.'

Emma paused and then said, 'I bet Tony didn't like that.'

'Not a bit,' Sally said, nodding. 'Whenever Adrian was there he'd always find an excuse to go and ask Lotte something, or move her to work in another area.'

'Then he employed him as Santa?'

'I don't think he had a choice. When everyone found out he'd chosen someone else, there was almost a mutiny.' She grinned. 'I've only ever seen a politician U-turn so quickly.'

'Do you think Lotte and Adrian were seeing each other?' Emma asked, picking up her cup but not drinking.

Sally puffed out her cheeks. 'I didn't think so, but you never know, do you? She was definitely hiding something. Others in there' – she jerked a thumb towards Fenleys – 'were gossiping and saying they were involved. She would have told me if something like that was going on.'

'Did she always tell you if she was seeing someone?' Emma asked, sipping her coffee. 'Was she even allowed boyfriends?'

'She's been out with a few lads, but it's never really lasted for long. There's always too much stress of Helena finding out. She found out about one of them and turned up at the café where they were on a date. Lotte was so mortified. The guy tried to make it work, introduced himself and asked Helena to join them for a coffee. That was a mistake.'

'Sent away with a flea in his ear?' Emma asked.

'More like a foul-mouthed rant,' Sally said, picking at her sandwich. 'Lotte didn't come into college for three days after that one. I saw bruises on her arms when she did, even though she tried to hide them. I feel so sorry for her. It's like she's not allowed her own life.'

'What life does she want?' Emma asked.

'Lotte is a really good actress and she always wanted to study drama at university. Helena never let her pursue it.'

'Why not?'

'It's as if Helena resents anything that takes Lotte away from her, even for a few minutes. When Lotte said she wanted to move to London to study, Helena went ballistic. Lotte never mentioned it again after that. Now she's stuck working at Fenleys full time.'

Emma raised her eyebrows. 'I got the impression that Helena doesn't even like Lotte working here,' she said.

Sally snorted. 'See, she doesn't like anything that gives Lotte the chance to be away from her.'

'What did she think of Lotte's friendship with Adrian?' Emma asked.

'She never knew about it as far as I know. He'd always make himself scarce if she came in. It's difficult though because she just drops in every time Lotte's working without saying when she's coming.' Sally paused. 'Almost as if she's trying to catch Lotte doing something she shouldn't.'

'Did she ever catch them?'

Sally shook her head and grinned. 'No, Adrian was surprisingly quick on his feet.' Then she frowned. 'Oddly, I got the feeling that he knew Helena.'

'What makes you say that?'

'It was something he said. Lotte and I were talking to him about acting and I said that she'd been really good at school, that she could do any part. Adrian sort of smiled and said, "It must be in your blood."'

Emma put her coffee cup to her lips and found it empty.

Sally looked at her watch. 'I'd better get back,' she said, balling up her napkin and dropping it on her plate. 'Was that helpful?'

Emma nodded. Sally's information had given her a hint at which thread she needed to pull next to undo the knot of the case.

Chapter twenty-nine

Allensbury Dance and Drama School was a shiny glass and metal building. It looked brand new and squeaky clean. Young men and women in tracksuits and trainers milled around outside. Emma weaved her way through them and into the atrium of the building. On her way in, she saw the poster stuck to the glass, advertising the one hundredth anniversary of the dancing school, which was being marked with an exhibition of photographs and memorabilia over the years. She smiled. Exactly what she needed.

At the reception desk, Emma was directed towards an area of the college where noticeboards stood, with photographs and posters from the last century. They were arranged by decade and Emma quickly walked down the row to the nineties section. She was peering at the photographs, looking for Adrian. She jumped when someone coughed right behind her. She turned to see an elegant woman in a ballet cardigan and a loose flowing skirt of what looked like silk.

The woman smiled. 'Are you enjoying the exhibition?' she asked in slightly accented English.

Emma nodded. 'There are some lovely photographs.'

'I noticed you were studying the nineties section very closely,' the woman said. 'Are you looking for someone in particular?'

'I'm doing some research into a man who was a student here,' Emma said, 'called Adrian Kendall.'

The woman nodded sadly. 'Yes, you're in the right place; such a lovely man. So sad what happened to him.'

Emma pointed towards the display boards. 'Do you have pictures of him?'

The woman frowned. 'Possibly in the other room. Come this way.'

The woman floated along with the posture, elegance and light-footedness of a ballet dancer. The scent of Chanel No 5 reached Emma's nose. She turned through a door into another space with more boards covered in photographs and memorabilia.

'You said you knew Adrian? Was that from his time here?' Emma asked.

The woman shook her head. 'No, I got to know him recently,' she replied.

Emma's ears pricked up. Could this be the woman Adrian had been trying to rescue? She could imagine him being in love with her and wanting to help her escape. From what or whom? The woman had continued chatting and a word caught Emma's ear.

'He was teaching here?' she interrupted.

The woman nodded. 'We have a children's drama group on a Saturday and Adrian took over teaching it after the previous teacher was taken ill.'

Emma was thinking quickly. That was two teaching gigs Adrian had, as well as his usual theatre job, at the same time as playing Santa. Was he that much in need of money?

'Was he at the class on the day of the Fenleys window opening?' Emma asked.

The woman nodded. 'Yes. The class runs from ten o'clock to ten forty-five. It's a bit much for some children – they're only nine and ten years old – but Adrian made it fun so they hardly noticed the time passing.'

'How did he seem?' Emma asked.

The woman frowned. 'He was a bit distracted, inattentive. When it finished, he packed up really quickly; normally he would hang around and chat to anyone and everyone. He was always popular with the mothers.' She smiled. 'He got a phone call as he was leaving. He answered it and I overheard him say something along the lines of, "Yes, darling. I've got it and we need to talk. No, nothing is wrong. I'll tell you later when I see you."'

Emma almost sighed aloud. There went her theory that this woman was Adrian's lover. 'What happened after he left? Did you see anyone around?' she asked.

The woman shook her head. 'No, not that day.'

Emma felt her chest tighten. 'You saw someone on another day he was here?'

'Yes. I was a bit surprised to see her, although it was quite nice that they'd obviously got back together after all these years.'

Emma's heart started to beat faster. 'He'd got together with an old girlfriend?'

The woman nodded. 'Yes. It was before my time here but it was quite the grand romance, I understand. It didn't seem romantic this time. They were having a huge argument. Well, she was doing the shouting and Adrian was trying to calm her down.'

'Do you know her name?' Emma thought this was pushing her luck a bit and she was right.

The woman shook her head. 'No, but I've seen old promotional material and videos of them working together.' She sighed. 'They made such a beautiful couple. She hasn't aged quite as well as Adrian though.' She smiled and blushed a little as she moved along a few photographs. Then she stopped and pointed at a black-and-white shot of a woman caught mid-scene in what looked like a rehearsal session. She was accompanied by a young Adrian Kendall. Emma remembered the picture of him from Joe Weldon's website.

The woman's face made her grin very smugly.

***

Dan was waiting in the car park of the *Allensbury Post* building when Emma turned in, cutting the corner at the junction with the main road and parking across the lines of two spaces. He walked across to the car and climbed into the passenger seat.

'What did you find out at the drama school?' he asked.

Emma pulled out her phone and opened her photograph gallery. She held up the rehearsal photograph she'd snapped at the exhibition.

Dan peered at it. 'Who am I looking at?' he asked, squinting at the small screen.

'It's Helena Clarke, Lotte's mum,' Emma said triumphantly, 'from about twenty years ago. When she was Adrian Kendall's girlfriend.'

Dan stared at her. 'His girlfriend?'

Emma smiled. 'And if my maths is right, he's Lotte's dad.'

Chapter thirty

Dan stared at her and then fumbled with his seatbelt, quickly slotting it into its socket, as Emma threw the car into reverse and backed out of the space at speed.

'You think he's Lotte's dad?'

'He and Lotte weren't a couple. That's why no one ever saw more than them giggling together and having coffee, maybe the odd hug.'

'Where are we going?' he asked, bracing himself on the dashboard as Emma had to brake sharply before pulling onto the main road.

'We've got to get to Lotte's house and quickly.'

'What? Why? Slow down!' Dan braced himself on the dashboard as Emma swung out of the car park, narrowly missing a pedestrian. 'Why do you think Adrian is Lotte's father?'

'We know he and Helena were together, and the dance teacher told me it was a grand romance. Adrian is ambitious and so he went off to London to be an actor.'

'If Helena was an actor as well, why didn't she go with him?' Dan asked, clinging to the handle of his door.

'I have a theory. I think she found out she was pregnant and she didn't tell Adrian. He took off and she was left literally holding the baby on her own,' Emma said, accelerating through some traffic lights that were about to turn red. 'It ruined her chance of an acting career and that would certainly give her motive, if she's held onto that grievance all those years.'

Dan frowned. 'It's a hell of a coincidence that he and Lotte end up working together.'

Emma shook her head. 'I don't think it's a coincidence.'

'There's no such thing as coincidence in a murder investigation?' Dan asked, quoting from Emma's favourite TV crime drama.

She nodded, eyes trained on the road. 'Exactly. I think Adrian only found out that she's his daughter six months ago. Maybe he looked Helena up for old time's sake and found out that she'd had a baby after he went to London. He finds Lotte and makes friends with her at work; that's why he was so desperate to be Santa again.'

'Must have been quite a shock for both of them,' Dan said, wincing as Emma took a roundabout at speed.

Emma nodded. 'I don't think things were going as they were supposed to.'

Dan slapped a hand on the dashboard. 'The plan that Adrian and Martin were working on was about Lotte?'

Emma nodded. 'One of Lotte's friends told me she was up to something and I think I know what it is. Martin's murder wasn't mistaken identity; it was deliberate. I know who did it and why.' She swung into the Clarkes's street and pulled up untidily at the kerb. 'And if we're not quick, she's going to do it again.'

Emma was out of the car and running before Dan had even taken off his seat belt. She reached the Clarkes's front door and raised her fist to knock. Before she'd even touched the door, she noticed it wasn't fully closed. She stepped forward and pushed it open with her elbow.

'Helena? Lotte?' she called. She froze as she spotted a Puffa jacket bunched up on the hall floor, blood spreading over the laminate flooring. Then she saw a pair of legs and a pale hand poking out of a sleeve. She dashed down the hall and knelt beside the jacket. Carefully unrolling it, she found herself staring into the clammy face of Helena Clarke. Emma brushed a few strands of hair back from the chubby cheeks and tapped Helena's face. There was no reaction. Then a floorboard creaked and Emma looked up to see Lotte blocking the front door, holding a sharp-bladed kitchen knife.

Chapter thirty-one

'Don't move,' Lotte ordered, but Emma ignored her, dragging off her scarf and pressing it to the knife wound in Helena's stomach. The woman groaned. At least she was still alive.

'Lotte, we need to call an ambulance. She's in a bad way.'

Lotte didn't move. 'No, she's finally getting what she deserves,' she said with a snort. 'Now I'll be free.'

Emma tried to control her breathing, eyes fixed on the sharp blade. 'Is that what Adrian was doing? Helping you get free?'

Lotte's face contorted. 'Yes, he was getting the money to help me get a place of my own. I couldn't do it myself, because she' – she jabbed the knife towards Helena – 'used to keep track of where I was going, who I was seeing and what I was spending. She never LEFT ME ALONE!' she suddenly yelled.

Emma flinched, expecting a further knife attack. Behind Lotte, the door moved slightly in the breeze from outside.

'Why did you kill him, if he was helping you?' Emma asked.

Lotte's face contorted. 'He grew a conscience. He changed his mind, said what we were doing was wrong.'

'When did you realise Adrian was your dad?' Emma asked

softly, hoping her tone would calm Lotte down.

Lotte took a deep breath. 'We first met six months ago. I'd been trying to find my dad for a while.' Helena whimpered and Lotte laughed. 'You didn't know I'd been snooping in your room, looking through your things for clues, did you? Anyway, I found a photograph of her and Adrian. I'd snuck out to a matinee at the theatre a couple of days before and I recognised his picture in the programme.'

'You went to meet him,' Emma said, still pressing on Helena's wound. The woman groaned slightly. 'Was he pleased to find that he had a daughter?'

Lotte frowned. 'He didn't believe me at first, then a couple of weeks later he came into Fenleys to find me. He said he'd been told that it was true.'

'How did he find that out?' Emma asked.

Lotte shrugged.

A croaky voice from the floor said, 'I told him.'

There was a moment of total silence. 'What?' Lotte demanded, taking a step forward.

Emma braced herself to protect Helena.

'He found me and asked about you. I begged him to stay away from you but he said he had a right to know you.' Helena grimaced. 'He had no right at all,' she whispered.

Lotte was glaring at her mother. 'He said that he would help me to get a flat. He said it was about time I had some space.' She smiled, her face glowing with the happy memory.

'He changed his mind?' Emma asked.

Lotte's arm went limp but the knife stayed in her hand. 'He said he couldn't hurt Mum again. He felt guilty about abandoning her when she was pregnant, even though he hadn't known at the time. After all his fine words, he wasn't going to help me.

He said he didn't think she would cope if I left.' Lotte stepped forward towards Helena, knife now gripped in her fingers. 'I didn't know he'd seen you, but that explains why. He said he was worried about you. It was just your manipulation, like always. Poor little Helena, such a hard life,' she said with mock sympathy.

'And you killed Martin because he was trying to change Adrian's mind too, wasn't he?' Emma said, conscious that Helena's blood was rapidly soaking through her scarf. 'He told Adrian that Helena had been hurt enough and that he shouldn't do it again.'

Helena whimpered again and Emma tried to squeeze her arm comfortingly while keeping pressure on the wound in her stomach.

Lotte's face was reddening and her jaw was clenched. 'He should have kept his nose out,' she hissed. 'Another one, in Adrian's ear, telling him what to do, taking my dad away from me.' She jabbed the knife towards Emma and Helena.

'You've killed your dad, and your uncle ... Are you going to let your mum die too?' Emma asked.

Lotte nodded. 'Yes, I'm going to stage it to look like she walked into a burglary and was killed in a struggle. By the time anyone suspects, I'll be far away.' She stepped forward. 'Of course, you weren't supposed to be here, so you'll have to go too.' Lotte raised the arm holding the knife and Emma braced herself for the attack.

Before Lotte could move, the half-open front door was flung back and Dan rugby-tackled her. The knife slid away along the floor and Emma kicked it into the corner.

'You took your bloody time,' she said, wiping her brow with the sleeve of her jacket.

'Sorry, she was telling a good story and I didn't want to spoil it.' He reached towards the door and picked up his mobile phone from the floor. He held it up and Emma saw a microphone symbol on the screen. 'I slid it in when you got her talking. I reckon we've got everything.'

Emma grinned and then turned her attention back to Helena.

'We need an ambulance now,' she said, easing the woman onto her back and pressing her fingers to Helena's throat. 'She's still got a pulse but it's—' Emma's words were cut off by the sound of a siren close by.

'The cavalry is already here,' Dan said, shifting his weight to make sure he didn't suffocate Lotte who was struggling to push him away. 'I thought we might be needing them.'

Chapter thirty-two

'What put you onto Lotte as the killer?' Ed asked, sipping a cup of coffee. He was squashed into one of the sofas in Emma's living room next to Dan, while Emma sat on the other. It was Saturday afternoon and they were killing time before heading out to Fenleys.

'At first I thought it was Helena,' Emma said. 'That she'd found out about Adrian coming back into Lotte's life and trying to take her away.'

'And that she'd done the only thing she could to keep hold of Lotte,' Dan put in, cradling a mug in his hands.

'Exactly. It was Martin's murder that didn't make sense,' Emma said. 'The neighbour overheard him telling Adrian not to hurt her again and to think about what he was doing. Martin was changing Adrian's mind. If Helena knew that, she'd be grateful to him.'

'You think that Helena knew about the plan?' Ed asked.

Emma nodded. 'When I realised that Adrian and Helena had been heard arguing twice – behind Fenleys and at the drama school – I knew that Helena wouldn't have killed him. All she needed to do was manipulate him through his guilt about leaving her pregnant. She seems good at that.'

'Only Lotte would benefit with Martin out of the way,' Dan said.

Emma nodded. 'I think Lotte thought that, with Martin gone, Adrian would just come around to her way of thinking. When he didn't, she killed him as well.' The image of Adrian dying in the snow flashed before her eyes and she rubbed them. 'The police told me that Lotte was about to leave with the money Adrian had given her so far,' Emma added. 'She'd collected about a thousand pounds. Helena came home and caught her. Lotte lost it and knifed her.'

'I can't believe she stabbed Adrian and Martin and just left them to die,' Ed said, 'and she'd have done the same to her mum if you hadn't come along.' He raised his coffee in a silent toast to Emma. She smiled and toasted him back.

'How is Helena by the way?' Dan asked.

Emma sipped at her glass of water. 'Physically, recovering nicely, according to the police press office, although I think the mental scars may take longer to heal.' She sighed. 'I don't think she's ever got over Adrian leaving in the first place, so him coming back and trying to take away her daughter, which must be how she saw it, would be even worse.'

'You think that's what Martin was talking about?' Ed asked.

Emma nodded. 'He must have seen how much it hurt her when Adrian left, even if he didn't know about Lotte either.'

'Do you think Helena wanted him back?' Ed asked.

Emma shrugged. 'I don't know. When you've held a grudge against someone for twenty years, it must be hard to put that aside.'

They were all silent for a moment contemplating Helena's

situation and then Dan looked down at his watch. 'Right, we'd better get moving. We've only got fifteen minutes to get up to Fenleys.'

Emma took the empty mugs and glass into the kitchen. 'I can't believe they're holding the window opening again,' she called.

'You can't have Christmas without Fenleys' window display, so Lydia tells me,' Ed said, getting to his feet and pulling on his coat. 'She's been stressing about it again.' He frowned. 'To be honest, she's been weird about everything. She said she needs to talk about something afterwards. I hate it when people say that.'

As he turned away to head towards the door, Emma and Dan exchanged a look.

'She's going to tell him,' Dan whispered. 'I'm glad I don't have to be the one who does it.'

'What are you whispering about?' Ed asked, looking back.

'Dan was just saying that at least Lydia has forgiven me for thinking she killed Adrian,' Emma said quickly.

Ed eyed her. 'I think she has, especially now you found out who did kill him,' he said.

Emma pulled on her coat and wound a scarf round her neck. 'Well, let's get to this opening. At least they're starting with a fairly low bar. It can't possibly be worse than last time.'

Chapter thirty-three

SANTA KILLER CONVICTED

By Ed Walker, Court Reporter

A twenty-one-year-old woman has been convicted of the murder of Adrian Kendall, who played Santa Claus at Fenleys department store in Allensbury.

Lotte Clarke, of Evensdon Place, Allensbury, killed Mr Kendall, who was in fact her estranged father, by stabbing him in Castle Park in Allensbury and leaving him to die in the snow.

She was also convicted of the murder of her uncle, Martin Kendall, who was stabbed in the backstage area in Fenleys. Martin died of his injuries in the Santa's grotto window display at the opening, in front of hundreds of parents and children.

Clarke was also convicted of attempted murder after stabbing her mother in the family home with the intention of leaving her for dead as well.

Tildon Crown Court heard how Clarke had been reunited with her father just months before the murders took place.

Mary Cusack QC, prosecuting, told the court that Mr Kendall had been in a relationship with Clarke's mother, Helena, when they were at Allensbury Dance and Drama School twenty years earlier. Mr Kendall had left for London shortly afterwards, never knowing he had a child.

Miss Cusack said: 'Mr Kendall had returned to live and work in Allensbury some years ago. Having found out about his previous relationship with her mother, Ms Clarke sought him out after seeing him in a play in a local theatre. Mr Kendall was surprised when he found out about his daughter and was keen to make amends. He was helping her, at her own insistence, to move out of her family home. She rewarded that kindness by killing him and his brother.'

The court heard how Clarke armed herself with a kitchen knife from Fenleys with the intention of killing Martin Kendall after finding out that he was trying to persuade Adrian not to help her.

'Martin had told Adrian that helping Ms Clarke to leave home without her mother's knowledge would hurt Helena Clarke all over again,' Miss Cusack said. 'He had urged his brother to make Helena aware, before supporting Ms Clarke's plan to leave.

'When she discovered this, Ms Clarke attacked him. Martin died in full view of hundreds of parents and children, having taken Adrian's place as Santa Claus. Adrian was absent, having gone to collect money to give to Ms Clarke to help her get a deposit for her own flat.'

She added Clarke had hoped that with Martin out of the way she could persuade Adrian to continue with the plan. When Adrian insisted they talk to her mother first, she killed him in a fit of rage.

In mitigation, Antony Devlin QC, told the court that Clarke

had experienced domestic abuse from her mother for many years.

'My client was under a lot of pressure, being involved in what can only be described as a coercive relationship with her mother,' he said.

'She was not allowed a life, forced to live at home, not allowed any friends and her money and mobile phone regularly checked for activity. There were also incidences of physical abuse.

'All my client wanted was to escape this relationship but took an extreme way to achieve that goal. The defence would attest that she was not in her right mind when she acted, due to the domestic situation she had endured.'

Sentencing is scheduled for next month.

A note from me....

Thank you for reading A Killer Christmas. I hope you enjoyed it. Please leave a review on your favourite platform and, of course, tell your friends and family.

The next book in the Allensbury Mysteries series is A Deadly Portrayal: *The stage is set for murder*

When local crime reporter Emma Fletcher is asked to help identify her friend's blackmailer, she discovers a link to the recent death of a teacher at Allensbury Dance and Drama School.
A police investigation is uncovering some dark secrets and it is clear that someone is seeking revenge for past wrongs.
As Emma's list of suspects continues to grow, the discovery of a second body puts her in the killer's sights.
Warned off the investigation by the police for her own safety, Emma decides the best way to save herself is to find the culprit first.
With the help of fellow news reporter Dan Sullivan, Emma must work out who is targeting the school before the killer strikes

again.

A Deadly Portrayal is the fourth exciting installment in the Allensbury Mysteries series.

You can find A Deadly Portrayal in ebook and paperback across all retailers.

Acknowledgements

Once again, this is the opportunity to say that writing a book, despite its appearance, is not a one-person process. There are so many people who have helped in the creation of *A Killer Christmas* that I'm sure I'll forget someone but here goes.

Thank you to:

My excellent editor Donna Hillyer and proof reader Victoria Goldman. Without these two, my work would never look as good.

Jessica Bell for yet another fantastic cover and Alexandra Amor for making the book look easy on the eye.

My friends in the Crime Fiction Coach group on Facebook. Your feedback on the opening chapters was invaluable and I was delighted that everyone enjoyed it.

My excellent beta readers, Jane Isaac and Mary Cusack (who also has a cameo role – see if you can spot her!)

My family – including dad Alan, sister Helen and her husband Paul (and Ozzy the dog), who keep asking me when the next book is going to be out, which keeps me on my toes

My mam, Margaret, who – despite no longer being with us –

is still the little voice in my head, urging me on

And finally to my lovely husband, Paul, who is always on hand when I have a wobble to say 'you can do it' and nudge me back into my writing chair

Thanks pet x

About the Author

LM Milford is a crime fiction author who writes the Allensbury mysteries, covering the exploits of local newspaper reporter Dan Sullivan.

A former newspaper journalist, Lynne's experience has influenced her work, although her stories were never as exciting as Dan's.

Lynne was born and brought up in the north-east of England, but now lives in Kent with her husband and far too many books (if that's even possible). She loves cooking, baking and holidays in Spain. She's partial to a good red wine and plates of cheese.

If you want to keep in touch and find out more about her work, pop along to https://lmmilford.com and sign up to her newsletter.

Twitter/Threads/Instagram: @lmmilford
Facebook: https://facebook.com/lmmilford

Printed in Dunstable, United Kingdom